Literary editor of the *Irish Times* for sixteen years, Terence de Vere White is also a highly acclaimed novelist and contributor to various journals.

Also by Terence de Vere White and
published by Futura

PRENEZ GARDE
THE RADISH MEMOIRS
MY NAME IS NORVAL
LUCIFER FALLING

TARA

Terence de Vere White

Futura

A Futura BOOK

First published in Great Britain in 1967 by
Victor Gollancz Ltd, London

This edition published in 1987 by
Futura Publications, a Division of
Macdonald & Co (Publishers) Ltd
London & Sydney

*All characters in this publication are fictitious
and any resemblance to real persons, living or dead,
is purely coincidental.*

ISBN 0 7088 2945 7

Printed and bound in Great Britain by
The Guernsey Press Co. Ltd, Guernsey, Channel Islands

Futura Publications
A Division of
Macdonald & Co (Publishers) Ltd
Greater London House
Hampstead Road
London NW1 7QX

A BPCC plc Company

CHAPTER I

"SIR WALTER WILL see you presently. Will you take a chair?"

The excessively self-possessed secretary smiled insincerely and returned with a valedictory waggle of her small bottom to the typewriter from which, after a short pause for self-respect, she had looked up to greet Francis Xavier Mangan's arrival two minutes before. The poet sat down, leaning heavily on his stick, and stared before him. The typewriter tapped, clicked and rattled away. At the end of each journey across the page it was pushed back with a precision which, after a time, put Mangan to thinking of the guillotine. Each time it was slammed back he saw a head fall. One hundred and ten heads had fallen when a discreet purr sounded on the telephone. Without looking, the frightening woman stretched out a thin white hand and lifted the receiver.

"Yes, Sir Walter," she said.

When she had replaced the receiver, she smiled her office smile at Mangan.

"Sir Walter will see you now. Do you know his room? First on the right when you come to the top of the stairs. Thank you."

The typewriter began to take its toll again, and Mangan rose slowly to his full height of five feet seven inches and arranged his coat round his shoulders. Bowing gravely to the secretary, who did not look up, he pulled open the door and stalked through it and up the stairs without remembering to shut the door behind him.

"Manners," said the secretary aloud as she revenged herself on the typewriter.

Outside Sir Walter's door, the poet paused to arrange his entrance. Then he gave a firm knock on the old mahogany.

"Come in," said a military voice.

"Ah, my dear friend," said the publisher, rising from his desk as Mangan came slowly through the door. He grunted and held out a limp hand, which the publisher overlooked. By this time he was beside Mangan, had an arm round his shoulders, and was leading him towards a chair. Then he went back to his own behind a Louis XIV writing table. He lay back in his chair, put his fingers together, and beamed at the poet again. Mangan said nothing, but stared in front of him like a cat caught in the glare of the headlights of an approaching car.

"Oh, I beg your pardon," Sir Walter took a tortoise-shell box and offered it to Mangan across the table.

"I don't smoke."

"Of course not. I forgot. It's so long since we met. Much longer than I care to think. Do you mind if I do?"

Mangan made no answer, but a slight contraction of his features could have been interpreted as an expression of indifference. The other so interpreted it.

"And how is Dublin?"

Sir Walter was still beaming.

The poet grunted and muttered something which was unintelligible but conveyed the same message as the spasm which had followed the previous question.

"I must go over some time. It's ten years since I was in Dublin. I don't suppose I'd know many people there now. I get manuscripts occasionally from writers I have never heard of before. Very promising some of them, too, I'm glad to say. But the Irish don't make novelists as a rule. Have you noticed that? Short stories, yes. Poetry . . ."

He nodded and smiled at Mangan who gave no sign. "But in the novel, who is there? Joyce, of course. But was Joyce a novelist? In a sense he tried to write the novel to end all novels. Very Irish, that. You are essentially a destructive race. And now I want to hear all about yourself. I wish you had told me you were coming over. We could have lunched together. How long are you staying?"

"I don't know."

"Then perhaps we could fix up something. I have to go down to Cambridge tomorrow. Rather a bore. Wednesday is not very good for me. Thursday—let me see. What about Friday? No. I see Friday is booked. What a bore. Next week, perhaps."

The telephone rang. Sir Walter apologised and then picked it up.

"Ask him to wait, Miss Tuffy, please. I can't see him just now. I have Mr Mangan with me."

Then he turned back to Mangan and beamed anew.

"This is awfully nice. What a surprise!"

"I have a play you might publish," said Mangan slowly, producing as he did so a fat bundle in brown paper. "It isn't all in type yet. My wife who usually types for me sprained a wrist. But I dare say I could get it typed if it were necessary."

Sir Walter almost winced, but, smiling instead, said genially enough:

"Readers don't like so much hand-writing. But in your case we waive the rules, I should think. Let me see. This *is* exciting."

With clumsy fingers Mangan struggled to open his parcel, while the publisher continued to look on like a bride waiting for a birthday present. At least four children's copy-books were disclosed, each with a dreary brown cover on the back of which a set of road-safety rules was printed.

Sir Walter held his hand out like a father to whom his first born is entrusted for sentiment's sake. Mangan, whose movements had been strangely slow until now, thrust the package so suddenly at the publisher that he dropped it. With a cry of dismay he reached down to pick up the papers. Mangan bent at the same time. Their heads came together with a sharp crack. The publisher jumped back; his eyes were closed and he held his forehead in pain. Mangan, unperturbed, picked up the exercise books and laid them on the desk.

"I am so sorry, I must have hurt you," gasped Sir Walter.

Mangan shrugged.

"I wonder if you could let me have an advance," he said. "I need money at the moment."

Patting his head with a white linen handkerchief, Sir Walter seemed to be pondering the question. Then he spoke slowly, as though each word had been weighed and measured.

"If I were on my own I would gladly give you anything you ask. My trouble is that I am in the hands of my board. It's very different from the old days when I could do what I liked."

"Can't you put it to your board then? I would like to know soon. I can't afford to hang round London indefinitely."

"Of course. Naturally. I do hate having to say this. But times are not what they were. My father would turn in his grave if he heard that the author of *Tara* was ever short of money so long as this firm was in existence. But I am in a very different position. The more's the pity. *Tara* was one of my father's favourite poems, you know.

'The grass that grows on Tara's hill
Springs from the breasts of slumbering queens.'

I know it better than my prayers."

" 'From the hearts of sleeping kings.' " Mangan looked quite surly now.

" 'From the hearts of sleeping kings.' Of course. How stupid of me. The magic of little words. The secret of the true poet, I always think. 'Then in a wailful choir the small gnats mourn' is one of the most effective lines in verse. But I am boring you."

"I wonder when you can make up your mind about an advance. I want to make my plans."

"Of course. Well, let me tell you what I will do. I haven't time to read for the firm these days. We have a pretty good team for that. But I will take your play home, run through it, and then talk to my colleagues. But I greatly fear—please don't misunderstand me—that they will consider a play should be acted first and printed later. Have you considered this? What about the Abbey? I hear strange stories about it these days, but I feel sure they would give a play of yours everything they had."

"They have nothing, so that would be easy." A sardonic smile, like a wound, now distorted the poet's face. "They don't want plays like mine. The Abbey wants kitchen plays, plays about corner-boys written for shop-girls. You want books about sex written by eunuchs for school-girls. I am no use to either of you. I can see that."

Anguish distorted the publisher's genial face.

"Oh, dear! Oh, dear! You upset me very much. But you must realise that present-day costs force me to neglect the sort of work we want to publish because the public won't buy it. How many copies did your last book sell, can you remember?"

"Three hundred."

"There. You see what I mean. I wish I could afford to publish only to please myself; but what can I do? We are the victims of circumstances."

"I am certainly the victim of something. I think I had better go back to Dublin."

"Please, this won't do." Sir Walter looked genuinely distressed, distressed and perplexed. He stared hard at his desk as if inspiration lay there. Then like a man who has decided to dive from a height, he lifted the telephone and asked Miss Tuffy to come up.

"I want a cheque for a hundred pounds in favour of Mr Francis Xavier Mangan."

"*Now*, Sir Walter?"

"*Now*, please."

Miss Tuffy wheeled round and disappeared like a pantomime fairy. Neither of the men said anything until Miss Tuffy returned with the cheque which Sir Walter signed with dramatic emphasis.

"I will be responsible for this," he said, handing the cheque to Mangan, who took it with a sense of relief which he tried to dissemble. It was the largest he had ever received in the course of his artistic life.

"Well, I had better be on my way," he said, and then, as an afterthought, "I should say 'Thank you' for this."

"Not at all."

Sir Walter was genial still, but when Mangan left and the door closed finally upon him the publisher rolled his eyes to Heaven and then sat motionless in his chair like one who has had a sharp stab of indigestion and fears to move in case it brings on another.

"The grass that grows on Irish kings," he murmured through his pain. Then he picked up the telephone."

"Ask Mr Colin Pangbourne to come up, please."

Mangan slowly descended the stairs. Halting before he passed through the outer office under the surveillance of the intimidating Miss Tuffy, pushing back his grey hair, settling his coat, his large hand held like a shield against his chest, he stalked through the door and across the office floor without glancing in the direction of the clattering typewriter. At the street door he paused for a moment to say:

"Good morning."

"Good morning," said Miss Tuffy without looking up.

And Mangan stepped into the narrow street, as superbly unaware of the traffic through which he walked unscathed as he was of the imprecations of drivers and porters on whose forebearance his life depended.

He really knew nobody in London whom he wanted to see. In the old days there were Robert Lynd and James Stephens; but he knew no one now except a few London Irish who would no doubt suggest entertainment. But that would be the old merry-go-round. How could he tell them that what he wanted was inspiration, new ideas, and the strength of will to concentrate on a full-scale work. That egregious and hard-headed publisher spoke for them all. Mangan had written *Tara* when he was twenty-five, and everything that he had written since was dull, polemical prose or lame verse. But because of *Tara*, only a few malcontents had drawn attention to the fact. American students and university lecturers dismissed *Tara* as the merest Georgian sentimentality, as minor in the Mangan canon as *Innisfree* in the Yeats; but no one read these learned writings.

Fortified by the cheque, Mangan gave himself a heavy meal in Simpson's in the Strand, saw the three o'clock performance of a film in Lower Regent Street, followed a middle-aged housewife up Piccadilly as far as Green Park Station without any fixed plan, rang the literary editor of a paper from a callbox and was told he was on holiday in Greece, visited Burlington House and was dismayed by the price of the catalogue, found his depression increased by the exhibition and wondered why he had come to the Academy exhibition when he could have seen good painting in Trafalgar Square for nothing, visited a news theatre in Piccadilly, and then followed a housewife from Eros to Cambridge Circus where she boarded a bus, bought the *Evening Standard* and entered a public-house to read it; and at eight o'clock took the underground to Euston, recovered his bag from the cloak-room, and entrained for Holyhead in the Irish Mail.

A young Dublin journalist recognised Mangan on the platform and insisted on pushing into the compartment. Seated in the furthest corner, he addressed him across the other passengers, arguing, pontificating, retailing gossip, its malice unredeemed by wit, in a voice like a rusty saw. Mangan's grunts, grimaces and monosyllabic replies had no effect on the younger man, who became more garrulous as his auditor displayed increased irritation. Returning empty-handed from a visit to Fleet Street, he was anxious to compare notes with Mangan, whom he assumed to have been in London on the make. There was enough truth in this assumption to make it doubly irritating. And when in reply to a direct question, Mangan said he had been over for a day to see his publisher, and the other, with a hideous simulation of laughter, exclaimed "Touch and go, what?" Mangan rose to his full five feet seven inches and left the compartment. At Crewe his persecutor discovered him in another carriage, sat beside him, and resumed his interrogation without showing the least consciousness of rebuff.

As a result Mangan arrived in Dublin in a thoroughly bad temper. Under the most favourable circumstances it is an exhausting journey, but with a tormentor at his elbow through the sleepless night, it was a foretaste of Hell.

The boat arrived at Dun Laoghaire at eight o'clock. Mangan made a dash for Ross's Hotel on the esplanade. His persecutor, who had seen him escape in the crowd, gave chase and joined him at the door of the hotel.

"Did you meet any of the *Observer* crowd?" he was remarking when Mangan turned on him, and in an excess of fury shouted: "Go to Hell. Go to Hell."

"Keep your hair on. What's biting you? I'm not coming into this joint. Not likely."

In this fashion the younger man attempted to calm his senior. Then, with a sideways jerk of the head, valedictory in the main, but pregnant with the threat of reunion, the journalist set off in the direction of the Dublin bus. Mangan had intended only to escape and had no intention of paying for breakfast in a hotel, but the scent of rashers assailed his nostrils, he felt in need of comfort, and the publisher's cheque in his wallet seemed to justify a modest spree. Had he met friends in London, or had either of those housewives whom he so listlessly pursued taken the initiative, the trip might have cost a great deal more than it did. So he went in and ordered a good breakfast.

Later he returned to his flat in Belmont Avenue to find the door locked and no one at home. This angered him—unreasonably, because he had not made anyone acquainted with his plans. In a sour mood he decided to call on a friend in the French Embassy. He, too, was not at home. Now greatly perturbed, Mangan set off to walk down Shrewsbury Road and take a bus from there to Kildare Street. The National Library, at least, would not refuse him a welcome. Passing down Shrewsbury Road he became aware of a face pressed against a window. Someone was staring at him. He returned the stare and the face disappeared from the window. Mangan noticed the name on the gate—TARA. No escaping from that. "My father's favourite poem." Pompous ass that publisher. And even then he can't get it right. Was that house called after his poem? Didn't that spiv O'Connell come up to him somewhere and say "I've called me house after you." Yes, of course. And that must have been the captain of industry himself with his nose pressed against the glass like a child outside a bun-shop.

Suddenly Mangan felt tired and old. His shoes were letting in the wet. He was going to the National Library. Why? He had read all he had wanted to read, written all he would ever write. What was the point of it all, this life-imprisonment in the semblance of a poet because he had once written a verse that caught the ignorant fancy. How much better off that man O'Connell, who had forgotten what discomfort meant, who was spared the eternal humiliation of dodging creditors, raising loans, begging credit, eternally looking at the cost and sometimes ignoring it at his peril. It would be nice to rest and not to have to struggle any more.

Rain was falling heavily as he waited for the bus, and two passed full before one stopped for passengers.

"Seats on top. Full up inside," said the conductor.

Mangan made an effort to ignore these directions.

"Full up inside," shouted the conductor, this time for the poet's exclusive benefit. He hesitated for a moment, hoping faintly that someone would recognise him and offer a seat. But Dublin is not Paris or ancient Athens, and no one thought of this small courtesy; no one, perhaps, recognised him. Miserably he climbed on top. The bus overshot Kildare Street, and in the rain, more intense now, it was a chastening walk from Nassau Street to the library.

The library gates were locked and a notice in a frame said they would be open again in a fortnight, after the annual holiday.

CHAPTER II

DANIEL O'CONNELL SURVEYED his drawing-room with uneasy pride. He looked at his armchairs and sofa in their glazed chintz covers with prim cushions sitting up in corners as though it was an effort to compete with the expensive objects with which they were surrounded, the satinwood tables, buhl cabinets, great Chinese vases, cloissonné bowls, and Persian rugs. These were assembled, as it were, to set off two very large portraits, one on each side of the fireplace: on the left, Daniel O'Connell in full evening dress; on the right, Mrs O'Connell, in black silk, by the same artist. The assorted treasures hinted broadly what the portraits seemed to state plainly. We are rich. We are bloody rich. We see no reason to keep the matter secret.

Although there were many chairs and the large sofa, there seemed somehow to be nowhere to sit down. The chintz and the hard square cushions covered with frills and bobs were intimidating, not inviting. To sit down on any of these was to violate them.

Daniel turned uneasily on one foot and then on the other until finally he came to rest before the painting for which he had paid one thousand pounds. He stared at it aggressively. It was long since he had given up trying to persuade himself that he had made a satisfactory purchase. The picture had been a meaningless mass of coloured blotches to his eyes when it had first been brought to his notice. Under tuition he had learned to impose an image on the canvas, to persuade himself that this *did* represent a town near a harbour and the broad squiggles to the left *were* fishing boats putting out to sea. He had allowed his wife and the earnest dealer who spoke in a tone of hushed reverence to persuade him that he *must* own this thing, just as twenty years before he found that he *must* live on Shrewsbury Road, and every day he found that he *must* accept invitations to the parties given by diplomats, and, in return, *must* give parties for them, parties to which his butties were never invited. Only Saturdays were free. On Saturdays, come wet or shine, summer and winter, he spent the evening at Milltown Golf Club with his butties, playing poker, drinking whiskey, and talking without regard to the claims of diplomacy, art or high society. He had stood firm for Saturdays and capitulated for the rest.

But he had to live in *some* house, and his wife could persuade him that it was an inestimable advantage for the children to have parents on easy terms with the floating diplomatic population; but no one could persuade him that he had not been made a fool of over the picture. After the first few days his wife had ceased to look at it, after a few weeks she ceased to mention it. It represented something that made Daniel secretly savage, a confidence trick, a great phoney act, played by people who wanted to pretend they were superior. Unfortunately it was impossible to show them up. This was what made Daniel so angry, this sense of frustration. He looked away, and at once his eye fell on the only picture he had introduced to that unlived-in room. It was a careful water-colour drawing of Ballybunion, Co. Kerry, an unpretentious, unrewarding little work, but very dear to Daniel because it reminded him of the first real holiday of his married life. There, he and Kate had spent a glorious month in the best bed in the best room in the best hotel in that popular watering-place. It was not their honeymoon—that had been spent, not without embarrassment and discomfort, in London—but it was what they called their second honeymoon, not long after their first child was born and nine months precisely before the birth of their second.

It had been a month of brilliant weather. Kate had consented to bathe and Daniel still remembered her gasping and laughing in the trough of the breakers. There were several priests in the hotel with whom Daniel played golf and sometimes, at night, bridge while Kate knitted or wrote letters to her sisters, most of them nuns, but some had married and lived in England and America.

The picture of Ballybunion had been bought from the artist who was staying in the hotel. It had been a proud possession. Kate in those early days never tired of pointing out that it was 'hand done' and 'signed'.

Dan at the time of his marriage was a national figure, a warrior, a senator and a tycoon. Immersed in the present, when his mind looked back it was to the hectic period of patriotic activity, a period very much in the background, but more flattering to his vanity than the aftermath, 'the chances' of promoting business that seemed to spring up unasked until that wonderful time when a policy of full protection enabled him to hold his countrymen up to ransom. Whether they liked it or not they had to buy the *Derrynane Product,* and when foreign competition threatened the monopoly, the Government always raised the duty, not for Daniel's sake, of course, but because a native industry was threatened. But the *Derrynane Product* was only a subsoil now, there were layers of other interests on top of that. Dan was on the boards of state-sponsored companies, banks, insurance companies, cinema and other paying enterprises. He had no interest in horse-racing, which was a self-imposed tax on the wealth of many of his colleagues.

Dan was shrewd, drank, but not too much too often, and genuinely respected money. He had no social ambitions at first. Kate developed these. It was she who called on newly-arrived diplomats, she who decided on the move to the over-large brick house in Shrewsbury Road, she who changed the children's schools for grander ones, she who eventually reverted to 'John' when calling her eldest son who had answered to 'Sean' from birth, she who eventually persuaded Dan to send the two youngest children to school in England. This would have horrified Dan in his early days, but somehow, imperceptibly, with increasing wealth, new acquaintances, travel, comfortable life, he did almost become convinced that he was a different person from the old Dan, that he belonged to a class of society which 'owed' it to itself to emphasise its distinction. Not that Dan would ever admit to a change of heart on fundamentals; if less fiery than in his youth, he was prepared without notice, at any time, to rehearse the history of his country's wrongs and to extol the fight for freedom. But he had new loyalties now, additional ones, loyalties to his class.

His gaze travelled to his portrait, a large if sombre work. The black suit on a dark grey ground contrasted but little with the flesh tints which were themselves vaguely grey. A glowing tip on the cigar which Dan held in his hand and a red carnation in the button-hole of his evening coat were the only touches of bright colour in a square yard of darkened canvas.

Dan was not a handsome man. His evening suit looked like fancy dress. The cigar had the air of a stage prop. Dan the patriot, Dan the elder statesman, Dan the banker had once been Dan the grocer. The artist did not let one forget this for an instant.

Kate O'Connell had been a pretty girl, pale with large dark eyes and a wide laughing mouth. Inclined to be stocky-legged and heavy-breasted always, at the time of the portrait she had become what an earlier generation called 'a fine woman'. Success had made her more formidable than her husband. When she walked through a room she gave the impression of one who is pushing through thickish undergrowth in a forest path. Her voice was loud, and her mouth, thickly painted and slightly drooping at the corners, had hardened with age. She tended to stare as if examining meat on a butcher's stall when confronted by strangers. The artist had been satisfied to suggest that she was vulgar. But had she looked quite different he might have achieved the same result.

Dan saw none of this. He was immensely pleased with the portraits. He was glad that all the world should see his wife in a Dior dress: and the large jade elephant with which her right hand seemed reluctant to play was as much a symbol of her cultural attainments as the thick string of pearls round her neck and the emerald and ruby rings which shone on her fingers symbolised the financial strength of her husband. "The children will be glad to have them," she had said when Dan wrote out the cheque for the portraits. It seemed to Kate that her children must share their parents' pride in the romance of their rise in life. And at the same time she was making sure that her children should meet only people who were accustomed to wealth, and who liked to think of it as an element like air or water, to be accepted as part of nature and not to be discussed or noticed with admiration or surprise.

Dan, most cautious in business, did not care to scrutinise too closely his personal relations, any more than he inquired too closely into the problems of religion. Obedient submission all his life left him at fifty-six the child he was at seven making his first Confession. The thought of questioning his beliefs would have horrified him, as it would horrify him to think his family was not united, affectionate and exemplary. His own relationship with Kate had undergone a subtle and profound change which, by shutting his mind, he had refused to recognise. The shy, laughing girl who had aroused his awkward, middle-aged, virgin ardour became in time an overwhelming mate: in this as in all other respects marriage had made her increasingly formidable. After the first two years Dan found that physical love was a short story which he had finished. This coincided approximately with Kate's discovery of desire; and it all happened without either breaking through the barrier of reticence with which they always surrounded the subject of sex. Neither discussed their relationship: both were prudish in speech and greatly concerned to keep their children in a condition of modesty which an anchorite might envy. Kate and Dan hid their thoughts from each other and, to a wonderful extent, from themselves. But unconsciously their smothered feelings expressed themselves, in Kate's increasing ostentation and Dan's sense of disenchantment at home. In business, on boards, hobnobbing with politicians, kissing bishops' rings, he felt full up and content; it was at home he felt empty and deflated. In bed his was the state of mind of one who travels on a train without a ticket.

He was standing at the window now. He could see across the lawn, over the boundary wall, the pavement on the far side of the road. It was raining a little, melancholy drops, perfectly in keeping with Dan's mood. He saw a familiar figure walking pompously along the road; a small man with curly grey hair under a broad-brimmed, black felt hat, and wrapped in a grey tweed coat worn in the fashion of a cloak. His trouser ends were frayed, his sandals, inappropriate to the weather, had not been polished for many weeks, and the string bag which he carried would have looked ridiculous with another man. But there was an air of infinite confidence in this man's walk which inspired respect; and his head as it glanced automatically from side to side seemed to acknowledge the plaudits of an enormous crowd.

Dan watched him enviously. He envied writers, artists and scholars because they required no support for their self-esteem. He felt deeply his own lack of education, and, as a result, exaggerated the blessing of a good one. With all his money and his power, he would gladly have changed places with Francis

Xavier Mangan, poet and novelist, walking in leaking sandals in the rain. Perhaps not a little of Dan's sense of inferiority derived from the fact that his glory as a patriot had a far less substantial basis than his success as a business man. Dan was at times embarrassed by the extent to which he had to pose as one who had given all in the cause of freedom. Like many another he owed everything to the political changes in Ireland; he had nothing to lose but his life and it had not been in danger often, and then not so much in danger as Dan sometimes, to cheer himself, pretended. He envied Mangan for his distinction; his work was there for all to see. His fame required no self-advertisement. Mangan with the string bag seemed to Dan, despite all the evidence of wealth around him, richer than he.

Dan, in common with almost everyone, knew only of one short poem by Mangan, had never read another word of his work, and accepted its existence on no other evidence than an assumption that it must exist. Indeed, his ignorance of his writings increased Dan's awe for the poet, whose head, Dan assumed, was full of learning and noble fancies.

Mangan was now quite close. He looked up suddenly, to Dan's embarrassment, for he had pulled aside a nylon curtain to get a better view of the great man. Now he let the curtain fall and retreated from the poet's lofty stare, humiliated by being caught peeping at passers-by from the window of his mansion. Everything that happened at home lately seemed designed to lower his self-esteem.

CHAPTER III

MANGAN STOOD OUTSIDE the library staring at the notice, reading hostility towards him in each printed word, while rain ran round the brim of his hat and dribbled on to his shoulders and occasionally down his neck. His trousers clung damply to his legs, and his feet in his sandals—which now looked like pulp—had suddenly become ice-cold.

Then he thought of Molly Pratt. Her flat in Molesworth Street, less than fifty yards away, had been open to him for twenty years. It was so long since he had been there that his conscience pricked him; but he had no doubt that if Molly was at home, she would welcome him.

As he turned away from the library and crossed the road to Buswell's Hotel, the yellow door of the house in which Molly lived shone like a beacon to a wrecked mariner. (Nor could anyone looking at Mangan have complained that the simile was extravagant.) A row of little bells at the side of the door were identified by slips which were mostly illegible, but Molly's, the top flat, had *Mrs P. Pratt* neatly typed in red and black. What, Mangan wondered, as he pressed the bell, happened at night? He often meant to ask Molly this question but always forgot to. Molly opened up with such a barrage of talk that it put anything one had intended to say out of mind. This sometimes annoyed Mangan, at the times when he was seeing much of her; but today he was grateful for the effusiveness of her welcome and the cascade of concern for his plight which descended when she threw open the door and found to her delighted surprise who the ringer was. Although it was a pity that he should come to see her again after six months' absence and catch her on one of her can't-be-bothered mornings when her hair was in a mess, her face neglected, and her feet in a pair of comfortable shoes.

But Mangan looked so woebegone that she quickly forgot

about herself and led him triumphantly upstairs to her tiny top-floor dwelling. It consisted of two rooms with a bathroom and kitchen. One room, which Molly called her studio, served to a great extent as a box-room and was more often used as a guest room than for any purposes of art. The room into which Molly led Mangan told a great deal about her. Her age—Eliot's and Auden's poems beside copies of the *Week-End Book* and *The Postman Always Rings Twice*; her means—the care which had been taken to make do with cheap but cleverly-painted furniture to fill the gaps between the few good pieces. There were a few paintings by Irish contemporaries on the walls and one, quite brilliant, but unfinished nude drawing in charcoal which Mangan always believed to be of herself, but this she denied. The idea had made him jealous once, and now vaguely amused him. The floor was bare of carpet but covered with good rugs. A bed on the wall opposite the window, covered with rep, served as a sofa by day. There were 'amusing' cushions scattered on it. Some Staffordshire china, a few flowers, two budgerigars in a cage, a few plants and indoor ferns, a print of Westminster Hall, and some relics of someone's residence in India, completed the furnishings of the room. A radio and a novel on a table suggested the end of the sofa at which the pillow was placed at night.

Molly turned on an electric fire.

"I was doing kitchen chores," she explained. Then, surveying Mangan, she added, "Take off those things and let me dry them. I will run a bath for you."

She left the room for a moment and Mangan heard a tap running and the complaining noise of a geyser. He stood at the fire doing nothing for himself until Molly came back and took his dripping cloak off, then his coat and shirt after she had run her hand round the collar. Mangan stood enjoying the attention. But when Molly went down on her knees to unstrap his sandals, he protested.

"Let me."

She stayed on her knees but ceased to fumble with the soaking strap. She heard his heavy breathing as he bent down to take them off. His big toe came through one of his socks. There was a smaller hole in the heel of the other.

"You need me to look after you," she said.

She collected the wet clothes together and stood waiting for Mangan to finish undressing.

"Could you lend me a dressing-gown?" he said.

"You have become very bashful," she said, and laughed heartily in the way that women and children do when life is pleasing them.

She threw him a striped bath towel.

"That will have to do."

He wrapped himself in the towel. This was all in pleasant contrast to his recent experiences, but Mangan did not laugh. Already, he felt, Molly had started to exact her price. This welcome, this bath, the brandy and milk or whatever other comforting concoctions Molly was sure to prepare for him, would be strings in a mesh from which it would take him months to escape. As he sat in the bath—too small, perhaps, for absolute comfort, but gratefully hot and refreshing—he heard Molly singing in the kitchen, celebrating her victory.

"I am making you an egg-flip," she said, coming into the bathroom. "Would you like to have it where you are?"

"I will come inside. But what can I put on?"

She went out again and returned soon afterwards with a beach wrap of pillar-box red, an Aran sweater of enormous size, and the lower half of an antique pyjamas.

"You will have to wrap your feet in a towel."

She stayed while he dried himself, as though grudging a moment of his company. He felt a dull resentment which she laughed at as a belated show of modesty. But it was her possessiveness which irritated Mangan. He had come in for shelter and had been greeted like the returned prodigal. An isolated act, an impulse, was being treated as a grand capitulation, a return to bondage. Soon she would be making plans for the future, looking ahead, committing him—not content with the present, mortgaging the future.

She settled him in her best chair and then squatted on a cushion at his feet. They might have been living together for years.

"Tell me about yourself, stranger," she said. "What are you writing? What happened to that play you told me about? Have your eyes been bothering you? There is so much to hear, I haven't seen you for ages."

Mangan did not find so much genuine interest in himself or his work that he could afford to belittle her enthusiasm. But mention of the play disturbed him. It had become one more bad cheque which he had failed to pass; he would have preferred not to discuss it.

"It's with my publisher," he said.

"But when are we going to see it? I suppose you wouldn't give it to the Abbey with the present set-up?"

Mangan kept his tumbler to his lips rather longer than necessary. He did not want to say that the Abbey had refused his play.

"Don't talk about me. Let's hear the news about yourself," he said, so uncharacteristically that Molly felt baffled for the first time since he had arrived.

"Nothing happens to a woman with four hundred a year," she said.

"You were talking about that antique shop," he said lamely.

"Oh that was years ago. I have been doing some typing, plays and stories. Nothing good. It often reminded me of you." She laughed somewhat hysterically. "That sounds very rude. I meant that when I am doing their silly stuff I wish it was for you I was working. You know I believe in you, Frank, don't you? I wish you would let me help you. You looked so tragic and neglected today. How can a man do his best work unless he is free from worry at home?"

"Carlyle had stomach-ache."

"Oh, Carlyle! Have you a spare copy of the play? Why not let it be done on radio first of all? Verse plays go much better on the air than on the stage."

"I have no copy at the moment. I must wait for the publisher."

"You are too diffident. I wish I could help you more."

Mangan had sent the play to the radio and had received a courteous letter of rejection. He felt his anger against Molly rising.

"Why can't you drop the subject of my play?"

His vehemence startled her.

"What's wrong, Frank? For God's sake."

And then he was crying with his head on her lap and her arms around his shoulders. She rubbed her cheek against his grey hair and murmured to him like a sick child, and he abandoned himself to her in his despair. They sat like this for an hour perhaps; the ringing of the telephone interrupting them at last. It sounded like a peremptory call from the world outside, reminding them that try as they might there was no escape from the bleakness of facts and the sullen face of reality.

As Molly rose to answer the telephone, Mangan thought to himself: "She has me where she wants me now."

CHAPTER IV

"I ENVY YOU that picture."

Maud Mountstephen stood in front of the thousand pounder, holding her chin in her right hand, running her necklace through the fingers of her left. It was her favourite attitude, perfectly in keeping with her slightly and deliberately dated manner, suggesting a vintage year out of the ordinary reach. It drew attention casually to her arms and hands, which were quite beautiful, hid her chin, her worst feature, and left her small but strikingly blue eyes to make their full impression. Her manner was so casual and natural it belied the suggestion that it was studied; but, in fact, nothing about her was unselfconscious. A sapphire brooch was calculated to bring out the full blue of her eyes. The general impression of her personality, casual charm and knowingness, youthfulness and sophistication, was exactly the impression she chose to make. She was no longer very young, and as shrewd as they make them.

"I am so glad."

Maeve O'Connell glowed with pleasure. She admired Maud more than anyone in the world. Their friendship, now in its third month, was the great excitement of her life. She hung on Maud's words, sought her advice on clothes, unconsciously imitated her—that trick of holding her chin, for instance—and confided in her to an extent which was unwise because Maud took genuine pleasure in gossip of any kind.

They met at Dudgeon's riding school. Maeve was a novice and Maud was taking up riding again after a long retirement. Maud had been well schooled and if rather stiff rode very correctly. Maeve was a natural rider to whom balance presented no problem. Moreover she was fearless. Maud was nervous but betrayed it so little that only her horse was aware of its extent. The two girls went on an early morning ride together before the general riding classes. At first Maeve thought Maud cold and unfriendly; Maud had found her attractive and admired her riding ability. The nervous strain of riding accounted for Maud's reserve. The rest was a figment of Maeve's imagination. In her own circle people gushed if they were friendly, and she mistook reserve for disapproval.

One day, Maeve having come by bus, Maud offered to drive her home. This broke the ice. And from that time the two girls often lunched in town together. On two occasions Maeve had spent weekends at Maud's house, which was on the north side of Dublin. She returned this hospitality by insisting on paying for whatever entertainment the girls took together in Dublin. But she had never invited Maud to her own home. She made innumerable excuses to herself and to Maud for this omission; all seemed to do credit to her sensitive consideration for her parents. At last she had to admit to herself that she did not want Maud to meet the family. No sooner did she realise this than she became bitterly ashamed and invited Maud at once. The fact that had so slowly dawned on Maud had been quite apparent to everyone else. It amused Maud, angered Mrs O'Connell, and saddened Daniel who bore no resentment, feeling Maeve's reluctance was but one more proof of her fastidiousness. He was quite prepared to be outgrown by his wonderful daughter, but Kate O'Connell was only at the beginning of her social career. She was full of ambition and what she lacked in confidence she made up for in energy. When Maeve thought Maud was snubbing her, it made her sad. (She was her father's daughter.) But Kate, in the same circumstances, would have become militant.

Maud and Kate could never have become intimate, but Kate would have been free of the inhibitions that kept Maeve from quick friendships. Kate was aggressive and without illusions. Maeve was a romantic.

"We are not having a party. I hope you won't find it awfully dull."

"We can talk which is much more fun. Are these your parents? Which do you take after? Let me see."

Maud looked at Maeve and then back at the picture. "I see a slight look of your father about the eyes. I'm not very fond of formal portraits, are you?"

"These are rather a sore subject. My brother and I don't

care for them, and my father insists that he only bought them to give us pleasure in the future."

"But of course you don't believe him. No one cares to admit there is pleasure in having one's picture done. There always has to be an excuse and a compliment about the boredom of sitting as though sitting for a portrait with an artist concentrating on one is not much pleasanter than a board meeting or a cocktail party, and most stimulating to the ego. That is why even highbrows are cross when their own portraits are not flattering likenesses."

"My mother and father are in tonight. We shan't be alone exactly." Maeve spoke quickly and despised herself for the note of apology which she detected in her own voice. It had not occurred to her that Maud would expect to be alone with her. When she went to Maud's house, her family was always there.

"And your brother—the youngest are away, aren't they—will your brother be in? I am curious to see if he's like you. It's always fun to meet the family of someone one is interested in and to trace likenesses."

"You look more like your father than your mother," said Maeve.

"Don't say that, my dear. All the dottiness is on his side."

"In appearance, I mean."

"But that is enough. If you look like people outside, you probably resemble them inside as well."

"I like Lord Saggart very much."

"But you do admit he is dotty?"

"He is a character. Only people who haven't to earn their livings can afford to be characters. That's what makes it so unusual to meet someone like your father. Long ago I'm sure there were far more characters in the world than there are today."

"You are quite right. If father hadn't been who he is, he would have been locked up. But Mother manages him wonderfully. And they have quite a lot in common. Father is an absolute miser and if my mother were extravagant I think he might have gone off the deep end. As she is Scottish and frightfully thrifty she just gets by. You must have noticed the wine was corked the last night you dined. Father was almost in a fit fearing Mother would point it out. I saw him signalling madly with his eyes when she took her first and last drop."

"I thought you were so sweet when you poured yours into your father's glass."

"But surely you realised it was corked?"

"All red wine tastes the same to me. It has an inky taste. I don't really enjoy it."

Maud laughed so much at this that Maeve began to feel foolish.

"I have drunk very little," she added.

"I was laughing at the picture we presented. Father drinking his own wine and mine to save waste. Mother taking one painful sip and lapsing into silence. You draining your glass in two gulps like nasty medicine. I thought you were heroic. But it is a curious thing about Father, he knows perfectly well what he is doing. You should have seen the look he gave me."

The way Maud spoke of her parents was one of the things about her which fascinated and slightly shocked Maeve, who suppressed criticism of hers, even in her own mind. Tonight was an atonement.

It was really on her mother's account Maeve had been shy. She realised this when Kate O'Connell came in and behaved exactly as Maeve could have foretold, with an almost ludicrous hauteur, a determination to impress so apparent that it was certain to achieve the opposite effect. And this was a pity because Kate, though coarsened with age, was still handsome, and had she been natural in her manner would have made an agreeable impression.

"Where is the Tio Pepe, Maeve? Surely you are not offering your guest the Amoroso. I am so sorry, Miss Mountstephen but I was out this afternoon playing bridge at MacLavertys'. Do you know the MacLavertys?"

"I—er. Which MacLavertys are they? I know—"

"Senator MacLaverty," said Kate briskly and continued her complaint.

"I find nowadays if one doesn't tell the servants exactly what to do they disgrace one. But I *am* surprised that Maeve offered you this stuff. Maeve really doesn't drink much herself, do you Maeve? That part of her education has been neglected. Her father must take her in hand."

"I dislike Tio Pepe, I'm afraid. Mr O'Connell will have to take me in hand as well."

As Maud answered, the wine connoisseur came into the room. Kate, unable to change the reality, had originated a legend. The husband to whom she referred in conversation was a myth of her creation. Dan the experienced traveller, Dan the gourmet, Dan the critic, Dan the moralist—the various roles in which he appeared in Kate's conversation were pure invention.

All this was apparent at a glance.

Dan looked like the rough block out of which an artist had carved his daughter. His hair, thin, greying, brush-resisting, had once been red-gold like Maeve's. The slightly blood-shot eyes were amber as were hers. And his smile, even though his mouth had lost its shape, had the diffidence which was part of Maeve's charm. Whatever he might have achieved elsewhere, in his own house it was immediately obvious that he reigned as a strictly limited monarch. His handshake was surprisingly formidable, and when Kate brought up the subject of Tio Pepe again, Dan resolved the problem, so far as he was concerned, by pouring himself a glass of whiskey.

"I won't take anything," said Kate as though doing penance for everybody.

The conversation until it was time to go into dinner was conducted exclusively by Kate on a sort of parliamentary principle, inasmuch as her remarks were intended for the general benefit but were addressed exclusively to her husband as though he was the Speaker. He preserved the neutral character of that office admirably, and of her three hearers was obviously the least concerned with what she had to say.

"I know you hate strangers, Dan. But I asked a delightful woman I met at MacLavertys (Kate never wasted a definite article on a surname, but spoke of all families as though they were business houses), a Mrs Pratt; I can't make out what she does exactly, but she is extremely artistic. We were talking about this anti-rheumatism drive—Maureen MacLaverty has asked me to go on the committee, by the way—and Mrs Pratt made a brilliant suggestion. It seems that she knows Francis Xavier Mangan quite well; well enough anyhow to ask him to let us put on a play he has written for a night at the Gaiety. The Abbey will be furious, but Molly Pratt says it's about time something was done about the Abbey. We can get the Gaiety for an evening. The only question is the cast. Mangan won't allow the play to be ruined by amateurs. You can't blame him for that. The critics will be over from London and, I suppose, like everyone else, he needs money. He can't let his play be botched."

"I saw Mangan this morning. He passed the house. He hasn't the price of a waterproof. I almost went out to offer him one, because he was soaked to the skin."

"I am glad you didn't. I don't suppose he even knew it was raining. Whenever I meet him in the street he is obviously in the clouds. He gets that from Yeats. Don't you remember the way Yeats used to sit with his head down murmuring to himself in the tram? He was never aware of the conductor until Mrs Yeats told him to pay the fare. Then he rummaged in his waistcoat pocket."

"He had a big belly on him. I remember that."

"Dan!"

"Tummy, then, beg its pardon."

"I must make a frightful confession." Maud did not look as penitent as her words suggested. "But who is Mangan? I don't think I ever heard of him before."

"But you must know *Tara*, Miss Mountstephen." Kate feigned delighted surprise.

"I am afraid I don't."

" 'The grass that grows on Tara's hill'," recited Maeve.

"That's Moore surely."

"You are thinking of 'The Harp that once through Tara's halls'. It is certainly very like. I wonder has anyone ever noticed it," said Maeve.

"Every child learns *Tara*. Where were you at school Miss Mountstephen?"

Kate was teasing now.

"In England," Maud replied.

"And have they not heard of Tommy Moore there?" Dan asked. His patriotism was always jolted by remarks of this kind. He had mellowed with age but was liable to get worked up quickly about the national grievance. Neglect of Mangan was the sort of thing of which the English were fully capable.

"I don't know. I don't move in literary circles. I can only say I never heard of him before. What else has he written?"

There was no rush to answer this question.

"I'm ashamed to say I've never read anything else," Maeve confessed.

"Poetry is not in my line," Dan admitted.

"Mangan has written a great deal as well as his poems," said Kate, frowning because she could not recall the titles of any of his works.

"I mix them up with AE's things," said Maeve. "They have titles like 'The Phoenix Flame', 'The Heart of Being', 'The Living Torch'. Not those names exactly. But something like that. I always meant to read them. It's like the National Gallery. One never seems to have time to go there."

"Plays are such a special thing. One has the knack of them or one hasn't. Have you ever seen a play of his?"

The sceptical note in Maud's voice irritated Kate who had been carried away by Molly Pratt's enthusiasm. Dan, ever loyal to his wife, and irritated on the national level, found himself becoming a partisan for Mangan.

"I think you would be foolish to turn up your nose at an offer like that," he said very firmly.

"That's what I feel. The anti-polio crowd would jump at the chance. Maureen MacLaverty says it will put their noses out of joint completely. I had to rush away then, so I asked Molly to join us this evening. You won't mind us talking shop, I hope?"

Kate's question neatly implied that Maud need not expect to have her opinion consulted when the experts got together.

"I think it will be frightfully exciting," she said, oblivious of having deserved censure.

"Why is Sean not here?" Dan asked when a ring at the door suggested the arrival of Mrs Pratt.

"I haven't seen the boy since Sunday," answered his wife. "I had no idea the medical course took a boy so much out of his home. I must speak to his professor about it. John is looking wretched, overtired and overworked."

"They are all inside in the drawing-room," someone in a rich Cork voice shouted from the hall. The drawing-room door was not firmly shut and the announcement was slightly disconcerting. Kate looked distraught and wondered what her new friend Molly Pratt would think of such informality. But the person so unceremoniously treated was not Molly Pratt; a young man came into the room and glared at Maud, whom he had not seen before.

"Maud, this is my brother, John," said Maeve, anticipating her mother who would have made a more elaborate introduction.

Maud smiled; John nodded curtly and then turned away.

"Where have you been, Sean boy?" said his father.

"I'm sharing a grind with a few other fellows," the boy replied.

"Why don't you ring up when you are going to be away at night, John? You have us all worried to death about you," said Kate.

John shrugged and threw himself untidily on to the second-best sofa with a healthy disregard for the fate of the silk cushions.

Medical students in the early years of their course are notoriously farouche, but this one was in some way exceptional. His tweed sports-coat and flannel trousers suggested work in the fields, and his heavy shoes, uncleaned, looked as though he might have trodden the bogs in them. He took after his mother, as Maeve took after her father. He had his mother's broad mouth and dark-rimmed eyes, her almost white complexion and raven black hair. His face became attractive when he smiled and showed his fine white teeth; but in repose his expression was morose. This was accentuated by an appearance of utter exhaustion. His eyes were sunken and there were tired lines on his face. Maud thought that he looked far more like someone after a debauch than an over-worked student.

The new arrival showed no anxiety to take part in general conversation.

"What's holding up the tea?" he enquired.

"We are waiting on a guest. Mrs Pratt is *dining* with us," Kate answered.

"Who is she?"

"I only met her this afternoon. She is going to help on a committee I've joined. I think you will find her charming."

"I must be back by 8.30. I thought tea would be at six as usual."

"Dinner is at half seven," said Kate with a glare which he was the only one to miss, being engrossed in an evening paper that he had taken out of his pocket.

Kate rolled her eyes, smiled conspiratorially at Maud, and accepted her son's resignation from her social efforts. Fortunately Molly Pratt's arrival caused a diversion. She brought a message of hope with her which provided the necessary relief to John's note of gloom. It had been for her a day of almost miraculous coincidence. A morning which began with an unfeeling letter from her landlord's solicitor, an appropriate message to arrive on a day of grey skies and downpour, had taken an unexpected turn when Frank, after a marked absence—Frank whom she had deemed lost to her—had returned without explanation but obviously needing her—or someone; and while she turned over in her active mind schemes to help him during the afternoon, making up a four at bridge—an engagement she had been sorely tempted to break—a wonderful opportunity had arisen, Kate's invitation was an assurance that the scheme for the relief of Mangan could be concealed in the scheme for the relief of rheumatism. Molly knew about everybody, and she had known Kate by sight for years. The meeting today had been a happy one; Kate had seen in the rheumatism relief scheme yet another possibility. It gave her an opportunity to enter the world of writers and actors, a world about which she had many illusions. Painting was played out. The least show of interest had been warmly encouraged, the dealers had made Kate feel happy about her natural discernment by telling her what to think, and when she had made a few purchases she found herself an advocate for all that was best in modern painting. But it was all too easy. One just put down money and learned a few lines of patter which seemed to fit every occasion. Dan had been only too happy to pay for the portraits. He had grown accustomed to paying for what he wanted. But he had quickly tired of paying for pictures which he did not enjoy or understand. It was like paying somebody to insult you. After a while Dan had said: "What do we want with more pictures?"

Had he really thrown himself into art as he had into insurance and employers' federations—matters which he understood—art might have become an avenue to a rarer type of social life than the O'Connells enjoyed. But on her own Kate found this impossible. Dealers treated her as a friend. She was met with smiles at exhibitions. A bearded critic even invited her to become vice-president of a picture-buying group which he had decided to sponsor. Her hopes had risen at that moment, but when she found that the group consisted of herself, the bearded founder and a president who never appeared or subscribed, it was apparent that she had attained a position of exclusiveness for the same reason that the boy stood alone on the burning deck. She paid ten pounds and fled.

Now came this interesting, sophisticated Mrs Pratt on terms of intimacy with poets and actors, and Mrs Pratt seemed to have taken an immediate fancy to her. Despite the formidable manner which Kate had evolved with prosperity, she was not at all self-confident. She pulled out her grandeur as a crook draws his gun. It was essentially a defensive reaction. She suspected people. She knew envy, and thought people wanted money from her. Dan had set his teeth against buying race-horses, which in his early days of prosperity was the way in which most of the new plutocrats displayed the gorgeousness of their plumage. Kate had cast her eyes more than once at the Owners and Trainers' Stand at Phoenix Park; but Dan thought the price of admission excessive. Art came later. The war put a stop to many forms of spending and, at the same time, made such people as Dan a great deal of money. Kate had three fur coats, trips abroad were impossible, motor-cars sat in garages, there was a desperate need for an outlet for excess earnings. Art, to some extent, was found to provide this. In the mood of the moment Dan gave Kate a thousand pounds to buy a painting. It made quite a stir. But that was the end. Dan refused to go further. After a while it became apparent in the art world that the O'Connells were a dried-up well. They were still invited to the opening days of exhibitions because their names were on the list, but they ceased to receive other marks of attention. Kate was frustrated. She needed action. Dan had an outlet for his energies. Kate had none.

And at the moment when she was most deeply aware of this, at a bridge party of all places, she had met this Mrs Pratt who had seen at a glance that Kate was a woman with a deep feeling for the higher things of life. It was a most stimulating experience, and particularly fortunate because Kate had become increasingly aware of the gulf that separated her from her elder children. John, whom his father so obstinately called Sean, never spoke to her except to ask for money or to complain that a meal was not ready whenever it suited his caprice to expect one. Maeve was withdrawn in quite another way. She was a thoughtful girl, quite unlike her brother. But she never confided in her mother, made her own friends, and by her silences seemed to imply criticism of her mother's ideas. Kate had been delighted when Maeve mentioned her acquaintance with Maud Mountstephen, and had resented Maeve's reluctance to bring the families together. A dinner, with Maud's parents as the star guests, occurred to her practical mind immediately when Maeve mentioned casually that Maud had driven her home from a riding lesson.

"Molly, my dear."

Kate rushed to greet her friend of the afternoon, who stood in the doorway taking in everything with her quick, bird-like eyes.

"This is my husband. Dan, this is—may he call you Molly? You won't think it too familiar? Where's the Tio Pepe for Molly, Maeve? This is Maeve, my eldest unmarried. She is wool-gathering today. Oh, don't say you haven't got the Tio Pepe out. Don't touch that stuff, Molly. Ring the bell there, John. Meet my son, John, Molly. And excuse his appearance. The poor boy is being worried to death for his medical examinations. And do you know the Honourable Miss Mountstephen?"

There was no doubt that some of Kate's exuberance was intended to chasten the Honourable Miss Mountstephen. It showed the sort of treatment that was accorded to those in Kate's charmed circle and rubbed in the fact that Maud wasn't in it, and that by her own fault. A knock at the drawing-room door caused everyone to turn.

It was the maid who, addressing her mistress in a stage whisper, gave tidings of dinner.

Molly Pratt saw everything in the colour of the rose. Just as she knew about Kate before meeting her, she also knew all about Maud; and she decided that Maud would be an excellent addition to the committee. The fact that Kate addressed her as though she were an envelope showed they were not on intimate terms—Molly was somewhat surprised to meet Maud here—but if Kate was shy, Molly was not going to let slip this opportunity to strengthen her hand. The more Kate tried to exclude Maud from the conversation, the more Molly concentrated on her. And Kate was at a disadvantage because she was unable to develop the Mangan theme, while Molly showed herself to be an authority on the subject.

"I hope Miss Mountstephen is on our committee," said Molly as she struggled to overcome a slight queasiness as the fourth course loomed up, gargantuan in scale like all that had gone before.

"I don't think we are grand enough for that," said Kate, who had been disappointed at the way matters had proceeded.

"No one invited me," said Maud pleasantly.

"I will tell Maureen MacLaverty. You know her, I'm sure —Senator MacLaverty's wife. You will know a great many on the committee."

"You will outdo the polio crowd before you've finished," said Dan, "not to mention the Soldiers and Sailors."

"I expect Miss Mountstephen is on both," said Molly, anticipating a gaffe.

"I think this is a very deserving cause," said Maud who had been genuinely bewildered by the turn the conversation had taken. But it is impossible for a sensitive person to be present when mixed motives are flying without being aware of the beating of their wings. Kate's social preoccupations, if strong, were vaguer than Molly's centre of interest. Maud had been impressed by her knowledge of Mangan's work, but as the dinner proceeded and Tio Pepe, extracted at last, had been drunk, for the sake of peace, with the soup, and this had been followed by hock, and in its appropriate place, burgundy, which in turn gave way to champagne, Molly, who drank all before her, became more relaxed. A false brightness came into her naturally lively eye and an almost tearful eagerness was apparent in her voice. And she talked at last about nothing but Mangan and his play.

And when Maud, who was circumspect in her drinking, began to question Molly in detail about the play, about which she had been expansive but vague, Molly's emotion increased. Her voice became dramatically intense. Tears actually started in her eyes. She gulped her wine, repeated herself, contradicted herself, and never completed a sentence.

"But I don't gather what the play is about," Maud insisted gently.

Molly drained her glass.

"It's about . . . it's about the whole modern situation . . . the betrayal of the ideal . . . the defeat of all that Yeats stood for . . . the . . ." She ended with an expressive wave of her hand which sent a jet from the champagne bottle which the industrious maid was offering at her elbow straight into Dan's eye.

Maeve giggled. John guffawed. But Molly, over-excited and rather drunk, burst into tears.

"It doesn't matter, my dear," said Kate.

"Accidents will happen," said Dan, mopping his face.

"She is in love with this Mangan person," thought Maud, who had suddenly become depressed by the evening and wished she could be alone with Maeve. How lovely she looked!

"I must be off," muttered John.

"Where are you going? When will you be back?" cried Kate.

But there was no reply.

"I am very sorry," said Mrs Pratt, wiping her eyes vigorously with a handkerchief which Kate had passed to her under the table. She had dropped her bag in her confusion. She looked frightened and suddenly old.

CHAPTER V

MANGAN PUT ON his clothes after lunch. They felt comfortable now, glowing with heat.

"You must go home and change at once," Molly said. "They'll not be aired."

She would have been glad to let Mangan stay, but he had been fussing about things he had to do ever since he realised that for the sake of shelter he had involved himself with Molly again. It was the last thing he had wanted to happen.

Molly had played with the idea of telling a lie to Mrs MacLaverty in order to free herself from her bridge engagement and devote herself to Frank, so woebegone, so broken in spirit.

But the hot meal, the warm room, the dry clothes, worked wonders. Mangan was clearly on the wing. And Molly was left to wonder when she might see him again. If only she could be of real use to him. But how could she help him with a play? It was one thing to be on christian-name terms with actors and managers, and quite another to get them to read a play.

And she set off for Maureen MacLaverty's, excited by Mangan's return and resolved to do something to keep him.

Mangan, his conscience pricking him slightly, left one woman from whom he had taken help under false pretences and set out for another who helped him with her eyes open.

"Is that you?" cried a cheerful voice when Mangan rattled the letter-box of his flat a few minutes later.

He did not kiss his wife, but greeted her with a familiar grunt and pushed past her in the narrow hallway, making his way into the room in which he kept his books and personal things.

"The room is in a mess. I hadn't time to get round to it. When did you get back? If you wait a minute I will make you a cup of tea. I put the kettle on just now," Bridget said from the doorway.

"The place was locked up when I got in this morning." There was a note of grievance in Mangan's voice.

"But, man alive, you don't let anyone know when you are coming. I didn't know when to expect you. What time was it?"

"It doesn't matter. I must get a latch key."

"But you lose them as soon as you get them. I'm tired of having them cut. Could you not fix one to your braces on a chain?"

"I don't wear braces most days."

"There's the kettle boiling. Hold on for a second."

Bridget disappeared, to return with a tray wonderfully furnished, considering the time she had had at her disposal. She cleared away some papers from a table with her elbow and put the tray down.

"Mind out what you are doing there," said Mangan.

"I wish I could get at this room properly," said his wife. "Tell us about London. Everything go all right for you?"

"How do you mean?"

"Did what's-his-name like the play?"

"Well, he could hardly read and criticise it during a ten-minute interview. What do you expect?"

Mangan was so accustomed to speak in a testy way at home that Bridget took no offence, and continued the conversation as though her husband was as forthcoming as she was herself.

"If he were only going to take it out of your hand, I'd have thought you might as well have posted it."

"I must go over sometimes. I must keep in touch. You might as well be dead and buried as live all the time in this city."

"I hope he will like it. But there's no money in it, Frank. The Abbey doesn't put on Yeats any more. The times have changed. It's a novel you should be writing or something up to date. But it's no use talking. We must each go our own way. Did you get a meal for yourself?"

"I did."

"And were you out without a coat this day? Let me feel you. You must have got soaked."

Mangan avoided his wife's outstretched hand. He peeled off his coat, keeping the slightly injured expression which he wore whenever he was concealing something from her.

"I went round to the library when I found the house locked against me."

"That didn't do you much good. I went there this morning myself to look up something about bull-fighting and I found the place shut for the holidays."

"What do you want to know about bull-fighting for?"

Mangan alerted himself to change the course of the conversation.

"A piece I was writing for the *Independent*. I went into Hodges Figgis afterwards and got it all in a book there. I hope the author never finds me out."

"I went to my sister's," Mangan lied. "They dried my clothes there and I had some eggs and bacon. But I had better change. These things must need airing."

Bridget got up from her chair and went in search of a coat, shirt, under-vest and pants, trousers and socks for her husband. He took them from her without thanks, and she served him without expecting any.

"I must get on with the article," she said. "Are you all right now, love? Your red slippers are under the chair there. I was half the day looking for them."

Bridget went back to the small typewriter on the kitchen table. Soon it was rattling away. In the next room Mangan sat staring into vacancy.

Two chapters of memoirs which the *Irish Times* had published, a thin book of verse, of which the larger part was a fragment of an abortive effort at a play, and an occasional review—that was the sum of his output in ten years: that, and the play which now lay in the drawer of his publisher in London, in a bundle with a box of cigars, a scarf wrapped in tissue paper, a theatre programme, a small tin of useful ointment, an ineffective cigarette lighter, aspirins, an old railway guide, a photograph of a baby, badly torn at the corner, and a copy of *The Times,* three years old.

He was not thinking at all. After indulging his self-pity this morning he was quite dried up. Dried up and dried out.

But self-indulgence threatened his liberty; every drop of sympathy which he wrung from that woman might have to be repaid by time service, by gestures of feigned affection, by a tedious campaign of lies and petty deceptions in furtherance of an intrigue in which indolence and vanity had involved him—

a tedious conjuring display, elaborately staged to produce eventually a rabbit from a hat.

He was in bonds at home. But bonds of another kind. Here was the tedium and safety of a harbour. Bridget made no demands on him, never asked him for money, or even enquired what he earned. She, from the ground rents her builder father had left her in his will, paid the rent, bought the food and supplied the deficiencies in Mangan's wardrobe. It was not easily done. The property produced seven pounds a week. But when prices rose, and her static income failed to meet the demand upon it, Bridget bought a typewriter and began to write. Within a short time she found she could place articles without much trouble, and at length she achieved a regular commission, a weekly article on the woman's page of a daily paper. She had no pretensions to style and very little general knowledge. Dowdy herself, she had no interest in clothes or fashion. But despite these handicaps she triumphed. There was a cheerful, motherly quality in her writing which, because it was genuine, never failed her.

Molly Pratt, who was kind and had suffered on account of men, shared Mangan's feeling that his wife was inadequate. Financial support—Molly had never learned its full extent—was not enough. An artist cannot live without inspiration. A practical, cheerful, kindly philistine cannot provide that. The idea that love had existed any time between Bridget and Mangan was laughable to Molly Pratt. One look at Bridget made that clear, she thought. Having emancipated herself to some extent from the conventions of her upbringing, Molly had become an authority on the subject of men.

An hour later Bridget put her head in the door.

"I have to run over to the *Independent* with this. I won't be back much before eleven. I left something in the oven for you, Frank."

Suddenly the thought occurred to her that her husband was dead. He lay so quietly on the table, his head sideways on the blank sheet of foolscap. A fly settled on his nose. He brushed it off.

He was sitting up now, blinking, looking like an old bear.

The hall-door slammed. On Mangan's befuddled senses dawned an obscure but, with the return of consciousness, an increasing sense of injury.

CHAPTER VI

"ARE WE ALL here, girls?" said Maureen MacLaverty looking round the table and, at the same time, beckoning a waitress.

"Coffee for . . ." Maureen went through the motions of counting heads. But it was only in play.

"Four," she added after having done an ena-meena-mina-mo with her fingers on which the symbols of her pursuit of and surrender to the Senator were symbolised by three bright diamonds and a narrow ring of gold.

"Is Maud Mountstephen not coming," said Molly Pratt.

"It doesn't look like it," Maureen replied. "You rang her up, Kate, didn't you?"

"I sent her a card," said Kate O'Connell in the slightly hurt tone which she adopted when Maud's name was mentioned.

"I am sorry if she doesn't. She can be very useful. She knows the right people. My friends are all the arty crowd who only go to these things when they get free tickets," said Molly.

"With Maureen and the Senator on the committee I should think we have all the social influence we need, not to mention Lady Kilmacud," said Kate, looking benignly at the fourth member of the party. This was a woman of very great age; her face enamelled white. Under a frivolous hat she sported a silver wig. When referred to directly she made a faint parrot cry. But most of the time she sat silent, moving her head from side to side, with the motion of a weathercock in a strong cross-wind. Mrs MacLaverty was responsible for collecting her, but held out no extravagant hopes from her support beyond the addition of a title to the committee list.

"If this is all of us, I might as well tell my news," said Molly.

She was in radiant spirits. Her qualms after the dinner at Kate's had been quickly dispelled. Maud, driving her home, had been kind and suggested a meeting in the near future. Kate, the next morning, rang her up and never referred to anything except the play and her private worry about her son's unsociable conduct.

"I have seen the boys," Molly proceeded. "They are both enthusiastic. Milton says he would love to produce. But, naturally, he wants to hear our date and see how it fits in with his plans. O'Leary was ecstatic. Did you know he had translated *Tara* into Irish. He recited it for me. It sounded wonderful. I don't know Irish, but he has such a gorgeous voice he would make a cattle auction sound like the Day of Judgement."

"Will he act in it?" said Maureen who found Molly too rhapsodical for her liking.

"I don't think so. He may be going to the States and he has an offer to go to London, and a play of his own is coming on shortly over here. He said he would love to, but he is afraid to commit himself, he could hardly be expected to, for one evening. But he does promise, if he is not in America on the night, to recite *Tara* in Irish as a curtain raiser."

"That is something," said Maureen, "but it hardly solves the problem."

"I don't think the Gate would be big enough," said Molly. "It must be at the Gaiety or the Olympia if we are to make money."

"Yahs, yahs," said Lady Kilmacud.

The other three paused as though considering this contribution to the discussion.

"We do need someone to collect a cast," Molly went on. "I wonder if we could ask one of the theatres to organise a week's run. The charity could take the first night and let the rest be ordinary business for the management."

"That is sometimes done," said Maureen sagely.

"Perhaps Molly will make enquiries," said Kate. "Does the author know our plans yet? It seems to me we must get his consent before we go any further."

Molly hesitated. "I wanted to have it cut and dried. Francis is strangely diffident. He has none of the aggressiveness one expects from Irish writers. He will only see difficulties. But I suppose a theatre management will hardly discuss the project in the abstract."

"Will you be able to get in touch with him?' said Maureen.

"I think so," Molly replied.

"Exactly," crowed Lady Kilmacud who was now sitting sideways at the table so as to see passers-by through the shop window.

"Would anyone like more coffee?"

"It's my turn now, Maureen."

"Not for me," said Molly.

"Only if you want one, Kate," said Mrs MacLaverty.

"If no one else wants any more, I think I should be on my way," said Kate.

"Yahs. Yahs," said Lady Kilmacud, which was tacitly accepted as a refusal by the remainder of the party who stood up as one, patted out creases, pulled down recalcitrant suspender-belts, thrust feet back into their torture, surveyed lip salve and eye shadow in compact mirrors, adjusted hats with little back taps, and screwed hair in where it had shown a disposition to stray. All this having been done, the waitress counted the consumption of cakes and wrote a bill which she handed to Lady Kilmacud (who had come out without her spectacles); then, at last, the party moved towards the door.

"It's my party, dear," said Maureen, relieving Lady Kilmacud of the bill.

"Exactly," said the old lady

It was surprising how apt her exclamations were, despite the limitations of her range.

* * *

"Where is Mom?"

"Is that you, Johnny? Nice of you to look your family up once in a way. Mummy is out."

"I want something to eat."

"Did you ask Lily?"

"She says 'lunch is at one' and she won't give meals at irregular hours. I just want an egg. Surely to God that isn't a lot to ask."

"But why can't you wait and have lunch with us?"

"I have to be back, I tell you."

"Back where?"

"Hospital."

"First year students don't attend hospital. What are you up to, Johnny?"

Maeve sat down and surveyed her brother with a new and curious scrutiny. Lounging against the open door, a day behind with his shaving, he looked like an escaped convict. Even allowing for the reorientation that first year students have to undergo, Johnny's appearance suggested some more radical origin. He was a year younger than she, and had been closer to her than brothers are usually to their sisters. This intimacy had continued after childhood. At school they wrote regularly to one another, and he told her most of his troubles. But in the last year, since he had gone to the University, without any marked clash or breach, he had dropped a mental shutter between them. He never discussed his life or explained his prolonged absences from home. Nor did he show any interest in Maeve's doings. So far as his parents were concerned, except to ask for meals which he consumed in silence he appeared not to notice their existence. A disapproving stare was the only indication he ever gave of hearing what was said at table. Kate gave facile explanations to herself, and accepted his excuses. Dan was worried, but tried to keep his mind off the subject. Maeve was puzzled and a little hurt. But her own life was sufficiently full of new interests to make her brother's defection less upsetting than it would have been when she was younger and relied upon his companionship. She knew about life from books, and wondered if Johnny could have met some woman who was 'dragging him down'. It was a phrase she frequently used, and Johnny showed no indication of having any uplifting experiences. He was attractive to girls. Her friends told her so. But he had never shown much interest in them; and at parties, when Maeve induced him to go, he had tended to stand aloof, glowering at everyone. It frightened Maeve's contemporaries, but might easily, so she reckoned, put an older woman on her mettle. There was something of Heathcliff about Johnny, a dangerous untamed attraction. He never drank and was bored by gambling. That allowed the mystery, she thought, one of two possible solutions—work or women. Work was Johnny's explanation. But had anyone ever worked like this?

He made no effort to answer her question, but turned instead to the side table on which there was some fruit in a dish. He ate it all ravenously. There was something indescribably restless about his bearing, as though he was waiting for a call and might be away at a moment's notice.

"Won't you at least sit down?"

"I'm all right, thanks. Do you think Pop would ante up now with that car he promised me for my twenty-first, if I were to ask him?"

"I think it would be a very tough thing to suggest. It's a wonderfully generous present."

"Cut the convent chat. I know it's a smashing present, but I happen to want it now."

"Ask him yourself. I shouldn't care to. He is touchy about things like that."

"Do you think I could get it off him before the weekend?"

There was a quite startling eagerness in the boy's manner, a ruthless selfishness which Maeve found almost repulsive.

"I don't think Daddy is in the mood to do you favours. I heard him say he was going to talk to the President about you."

"He will do nothing of the kind. He will make fools of both of us if he goes like an old clucking hen, worrying that man about his little son. I am not a schoolboy any longer. If Dad thinks he has the right to treat me like one, I will leave College. I'm fed up with the place anyhow and I'm more than fed up with the way things are going on round here. Mum is behaving like someone in a comic film. All this society stuff: what does she want with it? Awful people they seem to be, judging by the bunch that invaded us last night. And the joke of the whole thing is they will end by landing you all in a mess. That woman who got drunk—Pratt, I think—she is up to something. It's sticking out a mile. The other floosy is a quieter type. I couldn't make her out. But she is in some racket, you may be certain of that. We are not her sort. And it's time Mom realised it."

"Maud is a friend of mine. Mummy never met her before. What has come over you, Johnny? This talk of rackets and plots—it sounds so silly. Surely you have gone beyond the age of gangster films. If you want to know what's up, I'll tell you. Mummy is at an age when she needs an outlet of some kind. We are off her hands. The other children are away most of the year. Dad is engrossed in his business interests. And you must remember he is much older than she is. Mummy is still in her forties."

"What are you trying to tell me? The facts of life?"

"I hate you, Johnny. What has happened to you?"

"I haven't any time for your psychological explanations of Mom's snobbery, or Dad's philistine yearnings either. Look round you. Look at the bust of Pearse in the hall, the painting of Collins in the dining-room, Casement's autograph stuck up in the study—Dad's glorious past. And what has it all come to? The boys at Ampleforth in England, Mom running after high society, Dad acting the great tycoon and rushing to subscribe to the maintenance of a political party devoted to the welfare of big business and vested interests. It makes me sick."

Maeve said nothing, and after a prolonged silence her brother began again.

"And who, may I ask, is Maud? She looks a deep one to me. I saw her summing us all up last night. When it came to my turn, I was tempted to ask her if she would like to look at my tongue."

"She said you were attractive."

"Did she now? Am I to take that as encouragement?"

"Don't be so awful. I can't make you out. And you are being so stupid. The racket, as you call it, is only one of these charity 'do's' that most idle women mix themselves up in. But there is something different about this one. I am convinced that Mummy's new friend is in love with Francis Xavier Mangan. Her one object is to make a success of his play. That is quite plain. But I like her. I wonder what became of her husband."

"And is Mom going into the theatre business?"

"It is being run by a committee, Senator MacLaverty's wife is the chairman. She roped Mummy in."

"If that MacLaverty woman is involved, you need tell me no more. It's not fair to other snobs to call her one. She gives them a bad name. I can't imagine Francis Xavier Mangan having anything to do with a vulgarian like that. But I don't know anything about him really. I suppose you could write *Tara* and be a crawling sycophant. Just as Dad can look at Pearse every day when he is making out his bank lodgment and not turn a hair."

"What do you want Dad to do? Go about unshaven, taking away everyone's character?"

"There's plenty to be done."

Something in her brother's tone made Maeve, who up to now had only felt exasperation, suddenly uneasy.

"What do you mean, Johnny? I don't understand you. Are you—?" And then light dawned on her. "You are in the I.R.A. Is that the explanation of all this juvenile-delinquent act? Is that why you want a motor-car? You are. I know you are."

"Don't be a fool. And hold your tongue."

This was said with an almost theatrical violence because someone had come into the hall.

"No, Daddy. Mummy's out. She said she would be back for lunch."

Dan came in. The sound and sight of Maeve always pleased him, but he ceased to smile when he saw his son.

"Why did you run out like that last night, Sean? I don't know what our guests thought. And why haven't you shaved this morning? You are not going to sit down to table with your mother and sister in that condition. What's come over you, boy? I am beginning to wonder whether I shouldn't have asked the Archbishop's permission to send you to Trinity, if this is how you learn to behave in the other place."

Dan, like many men who have not been to universities, had an extreme reverence for them. He was constantly lamenting the fact that he had not had the advantages which he had given his son with such disappointing results.

"I'm sorry, Dad," said John, rubbing his hand over his face and affecting to be surprised at what he felt there. "I hadn't noticed."

"What's up with you, child? Are you not well?"

Dan went up to Maeve and put his hand on her forehead. He idealised his daughter, as he could not, with the monastic streak in his nature, idealise any woman whom he married. He felt for her a tenderness which he had never felt for any other living being, and a reverence which, apart from religion, he had only associated with his mother.

Kate subconsciously understood, and her instinctive reaction was to idealise her eldest son. For him she would have sacrificed the whole world. In him she saw her consolation for the failure of her husband to answer the full demands of her matriarchal nature.

"A bit of a headache," said Maeve in answer to her father, and pressed his hand. She was too shocked by her discovery to say anything. She would have to think.

John came back a few minutes before his mother returned from her coffee party. He had changed into a well-creased pair of flannels and a sports coat which was almost new. His shirt was neat, his tie carefully knotted. Above all he had a smooth shave, and oil had been applied to his wild hair with startling effect.

So great was the transformation in her brother's appearance that Maeve began to wonder whether their recent conversation had all been part of a dream. Dan and Kate, both anxious to believe the best, were equally impressed.

When Maeve came into her father's study to say that she was going out to dine with Maud at Saggart Castle, she heard Dan tell Kate that he "told Sean he could have the car now. It might help him to get home oftener". And Kate was so pleased with her son's apparent reformation that she forgot to look peeved when Maeve mentioned her friend's name and said where she was going.

CHAPTER VII

As MAEVE DROVE herself to Saggart through the depressing north suburbs of Dublin her mind raced and she could hardly restrain herself to drive carefully on the child-full, bicycle-bespattered roads. She *must* tell Maud. Just as it seemed imperative not to tell her parents a word until the problem had been thoroughly discussed and pondered: so it seemed essential that Maud should know it all and know it immediately. These imperatives indicated Maeve's age, experience, and the ascendency which her new friend had established over her.

"I must see you," Maeve whispered in the one moment she got near Maud before dinner. The older girl noticed how flushed Maeve was and the unusual brightness of her eyes.

What could it be? Not something to do with a man? Surely not. There had been nothing of that kind or she would have told me. She is a complete innocent. Her awful mother has made some gaffe I suppose.

"What is it, father?"

The last remark was made to Lord Saggart who was gesticulating violently from the fireplace. Maud's question had been pitched high enough to reach all ears, and it had the desired effect. The host turned away and Maud re-commenced broaching the gin bottle whose life her father had been anxious to prolong.

Despite the almost schoolroom nature of the menu, dinner at Saggart was conducted with a certain ceremony. Lord Saggart changed into a hideous velvet coat, once claret colour, now spotted and stained beyond recognition. A black cummerbund marked the spot where his waist once had been. His black evening trousers, now faintly green, had braid on one side, but lacked it on the other. A white silk shirt and very thin tie, like a bootlace, completed his costume. He looked rather evil, quite mad, and incredibly distinguished.

An appearance of having scrubbed her face with a loofah was the distinguishing mark of Lady Saggart's appearance. It was in keeping with her thrifty and rather neutral character. The only other guest when Maeve arrived was Dr Saunders, an impecunious bibliophile, whom Saggart had trapped into cataloguing his library gratis. This tedious and expert undertaking had been suggested to Saunders as in some way a national duty. He had accepted it in this spirit; a scholar, formerly in the public service, he had to cherish such illusions to stave off despair.

Dinner was going to be very dull. Lady Saggart would keep up a desultory conversation with her poodle which sat at her feet. Maud would sit in silence. Saggart, puffing and blowing in his Johnsonian, whale-like way, would shout unanswerable questions at the clerk who would consider them gravely before he mumbled noncommittal replies. Maeve could foresee it all and hoped that the extreme scarcity of food would at least ensure a rapid ending to the meal. Her anxiety was intense. She must *do* something about Johnny. And nothing could be done until Maud advised.

"I have made you a cocktail, darling. You are looking quite lovely. Did I tell you Merton Sandys is staying with us? He came this afternoon."

Maeve was too preoccupied to take in what Maude was saying, but it was made clear when the door opened and the actor came in—a man of forty or thereabouts, slim, with all his hair, though flecked (becomingly, she thought) with grey. He did not look like an actor; but like most actors, had a vaguely convalescent appearance, a deceptive fragility.

Maeve had never met a real celebrity before and wondered, in panic, whether they conversed in ordinary language. She was quickly reassured.

Later, lying awake, unable to sleep, when she looked back on the evening, she felt horrified at herself and the depths of her own selfishness, the pettiness of her character. The thrill of meeting the actor, his anxious good looks (although he did look older than she expected), his bromidic manner, his air of pleasure in her company, put Maeve's excitement on her brother's account out of her mind until dinner was over and the girls found themselves alone. Sandys had talked to her all during the meal; there was no general conversation. An unfortunate switching on of a radio set before dinner had let out the fact of a halfpenny rise in the price of petrol per gallon. This threw Lord Saggart into a great rage.

"We are selling the cars, Margaret. Evans must go. I can't afford it. I shall try to come to terms with Finnegan to hire his taxi when we need one. But I suppose he will try to push up his prices now. It will send up the price of groceries too. Transport costs will be affected. You will have to collect the groceries in town, Margaret, in future, and see that they don't try any tricks. If you go for the stuff, they can't charge you for their petrol bill. Do you know how much petrol we use in this household, Saunders?"

"A good deal, I should imagine."

"I should think so. We have the Armstrong Siddeley I bought in 1935, as good as the day I got her. Peter, my son, he lives in France, has a little, fancy thing. I shall advise him to sell it immediately. Maud has a car of her own. You will have to sell it, Maud. There are two tractors, a jeep and a small van. Work that out for yourself at the present price of petrol, add a halfpenny a gallon, and then you will have some idea of what I'm faced with."

"I pay for my own petrol, father."

"Don't interrupt Dr Saunders, Maud. He is making a calculation."

Saunders was in fact finishing off his plate of thin brown soup rather noisily, and thinking only with regret that the rest of the meal should, according to a menu which stood in a silver frame before him, consist of

Whiting
Cold mutton, cabbage, potatoes
Rice pudding
Sardines on toast

"It shakes you, Saunders, doesn't it? I can tell you it shakes me. I don't think we need open the sauterne."

The last remark—made to the butler—crowned Saunders' depression. He was aware that his host was using up a mistaken consignment of claret during the many weary evenings he spent at Saggart. He had no feeling of personal injury about the claret and accused his host of nothing worse than parsimony. But even sauterne with fish would have been a change; and it was disappointing to have to wait for cold mutton and bitter claret with a prospect of rice to follow. Perhaps, tonight, with this English visitor, whose name was vaguely familiar, there might be a brandy afterwards, perhaps, even, a cigar. Conditioned by circumstances to the harshness of the world, Saunders was thankful for small mercies and entertained only modest hopes.

When at last the women left and Saggart calling the men to either side of him said : "I have some port, or would you prefer brandy," all the clerk's unhappiness vanished. These were the small consolations that lit the murky path of a scholar and encouraged him to trudge on. His modest satisfaction was complete when he plumped for brandy and afterwards heard his host say : "This port is an experiment. My grocer put me on to it. God knows where he picked it up."

Lady Saggart disappeared after dinner. Her proud boast was that she was 'never idle'. Now Maeve had the opportunity to talk to Maud at last; but what she said as soon as they were alone was : "Tell me all about him. Isn't he fascinating?"

Maud smiled, but as one does at a child with a pipe in its mouth, or sampling drink from its father's glass when saying 'Good-night' in the dining-room, charmed by the playing at being grown-up, melancholy at the thought of the possibilities of the future.

"I hope you haven't fallen for him. He is old enough to be your father."

"He can't be more than forty. And that's the age I like men, when their hair is going grey at the ears. You never told me about him, that you knew him or anything."

"He's a friend of Peter's really. They met during the war, dodging active service, in some cultural cul-de-sac. It drew them together."

"You are too malicious, Maud. He looks delicate to me. And I am sure you are being unfair about your brother."

Maud blushed because she had been.

"Isn't he married? I'm sure I've seen him in the papers with someone. Julia Langtry? Aren't they married?"

"They are. As a matter of fact; it's on account of that Merton is here. He has been having a pretty bad time. Peter suggested that he should come to Ireland and take a rest. In France he would get involved in Peter's awful set. And that's what he wants to avoid."

"Has he run away from his wife?"

Maeve was quite unconscious of the eagerness which she was displaying.

"Not really. Julia drugged like mad. You knew that, I suppose."

"How could I?"

"I thought everybody did. She was always doing lines with impossible people—jockeys, labour party organisers, and even corps de ballet boys. Merton was very kind to her. Then she started over-doses and staging suicide scenes until, in the end, he had to threaten to lock her up."

"Oh, I see," Maeve's voice was flat.

"When Julia realised that he was serious she upped and went to America with some horrible little man in United Nations."

"They are divorced then."

"In process of being."

"Ah."

Maeve would have been at a loss to explain why she felt relieved at the news. Other considerations aside, a divorced person was as much out of her orbit as a married man. But, nevertheless, she derived an unreasonable, dog-in-the-mangerish, satisfaction from the thought that Merton Sandys was unattached to a wife.

"I see I shall have to keep a motherly eye on you. But it won't be for long. He is going up to Donegal at the end of the week, if he stays so long. Father makes it so rigorous for visitors that we will soon be quite isolated."

"Do you not think he is attractive, Maud?"

"Merton? Oh, I hadn't thought about it. I suppose he is. I don't care for actors. They gush so. And they are always thinking about themselves and their careers. They are rather like gold-digging girls."

Maeve, who had never met anyone to compare with Merton, paused as though considering Maud's remark.

"I don't suppose I like them as a rule either."

She had never met any.

"But I think he is different," she added. "I should never have thought he was an actor. And he never talked about himself at all. Had he been like the boys I meet he would have gone on and on about himself or his hobbies and left me in the air. You have no idea what it's like to be a girl in Dublin. I mean... perhaps you don't know what I mean. You came out in London, and you didn't have to spend your time with first year medical students and the sons of Daddy's friends."

"Merton is a man of the world. And I do agree he has charming manners. It's only that as a type I don't care for actors. But what you say about the young men you meet goes for all young men. I shall never forget some of the experiences of the year I came out. And then hunt balls... and tipsy old men. The young ones usually pass out. It shows how tough women are fundamentally that they don't retire *en masse* to convents after their debutante year."

Maeve was not in a mood for generalisations, so that Maud's observations were, in effect, a soliloquy. It served as a musical background to Maeve's thoughts which now with a spasm of guilt turned back to her brother. She had quite forgotten him.

"There is something much more important than Merton Sandys to talk about, Maud. It's absolutely secret. No one knows about it. But I must talk to someone and decide what to do. You won't breathe a word, will you?"

"Of course not."

"It's about Johnny. I only found out today. You know he is behaving very strangely. You saw him last night. I don't know why I didn't guess. He's in the I.R.A."

"In the what?"

"The I.R.A. He is one of the people who make attacks on the Border."

"But how exciting!"

"How can you say that? He may be caught and sent to prison for years. If someone is killed, he may be executed. And, quite apart from that, it makes him obsessed and mad. It twists his mind. It's all wrong and uncivilised and crazy. But what am I to do?"

"Where's your mother, Maud?"

The girls looked up to see that Lord Saggart and Merton

Sandys had come into the room. Saggart had bellowed his question from the end of the room; there was no fear that Maeve had been overheard.

"She said she was getting things ready for a sale. I think she must be up in the sewing-room."

"She never rests. Margaret doesn't. It would kill any other woman. It's in the blood. Her mother rode a bicycle when she was ninety. And her grandfather had a bastard when he was eighty-five. I hope you take after her, Maud. I'm afraid Peter won't."

"Where is Mr Saunders, Poppa?"

"He had to go off. Afraid of missing his bus."

"You didn't let him go off in this rain."

"Won't do him any harm. We will all have to get used to it soon when the cars go."

"I would have driven him home," said Maeve.

"He's used to the bus. Prefers it probably. Funny chap. Noses round the library here, day after day. Gets some amusement out of it, I suppose. Not my idea of amusement. I wonder would he buy the Armstrong Siddeley? He hasn't got a car. I would sell it for three hundred pounds."

"You'd better ask him, father. I should imagine three hundred pounds represents a year's pension. But I don't think the question will arise. He is bound to catch pneumonia walking down the avenue in this."

The rain was lashing against the windows and falling in regular heavy drops down the chimney.

Everyone thought about Mr Saunders out in the rain. Everyone, that is to say, except Lord Saggart, who interrupted the silence to say: "I am going to bed. Better conserve my energies if I have to take to walking again. You know your room, Sandys. You won't want a nightcap will you? I've locked up the sideboard."

"I have done very well. Thank you."

"Glad to hear you say so. My! That port was awful stuff, wasn't it? Did you finish yours? I shall have a few words with that grocer fellow. Landed me with a dozen. I suppose he will take them back. He'd better. Saunders was lucky. He stuck to the brandy. That fire looks very bad. Don't sit up late. You'll catch your deaths of cold."

With that his lordship turned abruptly about and walked very rapidly out of the room. At the door he paused as though to say something, thought better of it, and went on. His thought must have amused him for a loud peal of laughter rang out in the passage, and again on the stairs, and on the landing upstairs, and later in the night, when it woke all who slept in the principal bedrooms and filled them with alarm.

"Come along," said Maud as soon as her father's laughter died away. Maeve and Merton followed her across the inter-communicating drawing-rooms into a small room in the tower around which the mansion was built. It was comfortably furnished. A log fire crackled in the grate and a reassuring supply of bottles and tumblers stood on a table in the corner. Maeve sat on a low chair, Merton lolled on a small sofa, Maud crouched, cat-like, on the hearth rug. The fire threw vague but comforting shadows on the wall. The thick curtains kept out the harshness of the night, and muffled the spatter of the rain on the windows and the wail of the storm. The wildness outside only emphasised the comfort within.

Rubbing her hands round the bowl of the brandy glass, arching her back slightly and gazing into the flames, Maud said:

"Go on about your brother, darling. Listen to this, Merton."

Maeve felt a pang of disappointment and a sudden rush of misgiving. How could Maud treat so casually such a confidence? Much that had seemed cold and hard in Maud's manner she had passed over as a superficial crust which was part of the legacy of high breeding. But nothing could explain this indifference to her feelings. And because she was so infatuated by Maud her disappointment was the more intense. And she had had, by any standards, an exacting day.

"Maud, please."

She could not say more. Indeed the effort to say this was too much. To her dismay she felt tears in her eyes. And she knew that they had been in her voice.

"Darling, what's the matter?"

"I told you it was a secret. Don't you understand? It's most terribly serious."

"But Merton is an old friend. He doesn't know about what goes on here, or who you are talking about."

"Don't worry about me," said Merton putting a fatherly hand

on Maeve's shoulder. "But in any event I will leave you girls to it. I have had a long day and flying always tired me. And I am threatened with a walk to Donegal on account of this halfpenny petrol crisis. Good-night, Maud, darling."

He pecked the cheek which Maud extended.

"Good-night, Maeve. Shall I see you tomorrow?"

"I'm afraid not."

"Yes you will. Maeve is going to stay the night. We have a lot to talk about and I won't let her drive home in this storm."

"Good, I'll see you, then."

He, too, paused at the door.

"Poor Mr Saunders," he said. "Was that what made your father laugh so much?"

"I have given up trying to understand my father. But I think it's most likely."

When Merton shut the door behind him, Maud pulled Maeve, who was reluctant at first, down beside her, petted and stroked her like a child and kissed first her eyes and then her forehead very gently.

Maeve felt at first somewhat surprised and confused by this. But after the apparent unkindness that had preceded it, she was relieved. And, after a while, relaxed in the comfort and quiet, the fire glow and Maud's gentle, insistent voice which seemed in some way Maeve could not exactly define to come from another and more mysterious person than the detached and casual Maud whose interest had flattered her so much, she felt at peace again.

"I am so worried about Johnny."

"I know, darling. But don't worry. We will talk about it in the morning. What pretty hands you have. Let me see."

There was something so compelling in Maud's manner that Maeve did really feel that the problem of Johnny was safe in her charge, and that she would provide a solution. So completely had Maeve surrendered to the personality of the older woman that she did cease to worry about her brother, and lying at the fire, her head on Maud's shoulder, her mind turned to happier themes. She was smiling when she said:

"Is he very susceptible to women?"

"Who?"

There was such an unexpected sharpness in the way Maud

uttered the question that Maeve when she said, "Merton, I mean," hurried to change the subject. But Maud was not to be appeased. Her whole body seemed to freeze, and Maeve sat up. feeling suddenly repulsed. It was certainly quite a business getting to know people. One could never be sure how they were going to take things.

CHAPTER VIII

A WOOD-PIGEON, VERY persistent, broke in on Maeve's dream, where it had become Mother Rita at the convent, saying "Get up, get up, get up"—and awoke her at last. It took her a little time to realise where she was. She had woken once in the night, the wind became a gale and rattled the window mercilessly. But that sound, too, had been confused by another inside the house—Lord Saggart recollecting his private joke.

At home Maeve would have jumped out of bed. In this house she lay, very wide awake, until the maid came in with early tea and pulled back the curtains. The sun, in a pale blue sky, poured into the room. Like a murderer who has washed away all traces of his crime, it was difficult to reconcile the genial welcome of the morning with the savagery of the night. But the change was a happy augury. Maeve had unbounded confidence in Maud's capacity and she had been touched and somewhat surprised by her excessive solicitude last night. And why did she become so touchy all of a sudden? Not that Maeve was happy about the demonstration of tenderness that preceded it. "Soppy" she called it. She did not like demonstrativeness. It was one of her mother's characteristics that most alienated her sympathy. Boys who wanted to make headway with Maeve ruined their chances when they became intense. It had been an astonishing display from Maud, Maud who was so cool and dignified that she made all impulsiveness and enthusiasm seem rather common. Perhaps she had some love affair of her own that she was brooding over. But if she had surely she would have hinted at it before this. Maeve felt ashamed of the way she had comported herself. She had been such a baby to cry. It made her feel very embarrassed at the prospect of facing Merton Sandys again. But she had not cried much, a few tears. He would understand. Anyhow, the prospect of *not* meeting him was worse.

She took a very quick dip in a shallow bath and arrived in the dining-room first. Somehow she felt quite certain that Lady Saggart, in keeping with her general character, would be next; and it came as a complete surprise when Merton, dressed for the country, came in. He was as easy and natural in the morning as he had been at dinner. Without being witty, he had a funny way of putting things, a light, self-mocking manner, unlike anything Maeve had met before. The men in her life had always taken themselves rather ponderously. But the most entrancing aspect of Merton's manner was the flattering way in which he seemed all the time to be aware of Maeve, to include her in what he was saying. It was such a change from what she was accustomed to: being lectured or ignored, and given to understand that women played a subsidiary part in the divine plan.

Merton was the most celebrated person that Maeve had ever met, but he made her feel important and attractive. By the time she had taken her second cup of coffee, she loved him, she knew, for ever.

"Are you going to Dublin this morning?" he asked.

"I am, immediately after breakfast."

"Would you have room for me in your car? I must do some shopping and get my hair cut."

"I would be delighted to have your company."

This conversation took place before Maud joined them. She came down in old slacks and an unbecoming jumper. Her face was drawn. She had not been able to sleep with the storm and the laughter from her father's room which had shaken the house, she said.

"I need not ask how you slept," she said, looking at Maeve with a tolerant expression with which an adult overlooks the innocent insensitivity of a child.

"She looks smashing. Doesn't she?" said Merton.

"He means you, darling," said Maud, helping herself slowly to kidneys.

"Maeve is very kindly driving me to Dublin," he added.

"There's no need to go up so soon. The car, despite father, will be going in before lunch."

"Perhaps I could get a lift home. But I left so much undone in town—I came away in such a scramble, I would like to have a full morning in Dublin. But I don't want to hurry Maeve."

"I must go anyway. I have a class in the School of Art at eleven. What about you, Maud?"

"I am not exactly dressed for Dublin. Don't forget we are dining out tonight, Merton, in case you took it into your head to visit Mr Saunders in hospital."

"I feel so guilty about him," said Maeve.

"Judging by father's high spirits, he does not share your remorse. Did he not wake you at about four o'clock? I never heard anything like it. I thought at first that the gale had blown in the conservatory window."

* * *

Driving away from Saggart Maeve felt twinges of guilt. Her mother had been monosyllabic when she rang up to explain why she had not come home. Maud had been curiously absent in manner, and when Maeve had said "We haven't come to any decision about Johnny", Maud replied : "I'd talk to your parents if I were you," and then began to read the paper with such a fever of concentration that Maeve almost felt she intended to snub her. But why? Maud was certainly a most unpredictable person when one got to know her.

In the car Maeve played with the idea of taking Merton into her confidence, but dismissed it as an unworthy desire to kill two birds with one stone. Instead she carried out a pleasant, bantering conversation. It would be time enough to deal with Johnny's problem when she got home. Merton got out at a barber's.

"When is your class over?" he asked.

"One."

"Could we lunch together somewhere?"

"Let me see . . . I'm afraid I must . . . I'm expected at home. I am so sorry."

"Ring up home and say you will be back in time for tea."

"No but seriously. Oh, very well. I shouldn't but I'd love to."

"Jammets then at 1.15."

Throughout her art class Maeve's mind was not strictly on her work. She was not in any event particularly gifted : her talent was such as Victorians displayed in water-colour records of holiday trips or flower gardens, records they were content to keep with medals and letters as part of the paraphernalia of home. She had no definite plan. She had been abroad in a convent, so secluded that she would have been much better at home; and after that tantalising year of glimpses of Paris as through a prison window, she had been allowed to take a year off before deciding what she would do. So far as Dan was concerned, and he would have preferred it so, there was no need for her to work at all.

A certain reserve in Maeve's manner, the result of a sudden misgiving, made the beginning of the luncheon rather stickier than either had expected. But this was negotiated tactfully by Merton, who guessed a headache as the cause; and it was only the gradual realisation that the restaurant was empty and the waiters standing patiently in the wings brought them to a realisation of how swiftly time had passed. The Saggart car was forgotten. Maeve drove as far as the gate lodge and put Merton down there. Then she drove home feeling as though she was moving effortlessly in a new element out of touch with humankind, invulnerable, enchanted. She had told Merton a great deal. He could fill in any gaps and complete the portrait if he pleased. About him she still knew very little. Not that he seemed reticent or avoided any questions: he conversed without reference to himself and kept Maeve in the centre of the conversation. She told him what Dublin was like for a girl of her age. Boys gathered together at one end of a room, girls at the other. If a boy took a fancy to one he followed either of two courses: if timid he made an immediate avowal of love, after the first dance and before the conversation had developed further than mutual assurances about the quality of the band and the merits of the floor; if bold or, at least, reckless, he adopted the tactics of the quick-minded when they see a child walk under traffic—a dive, unheralded, a frantic snatch, and hope for the best. Then there were the more sophisticated types who spent the evening in the bar and expected to end an evening in which the girl had been neglected with a petting routine, depressing, mechanical and anonymous.

It was after this that Merton had asked casually:

"Are you a great friend of Maud's?"

"She has been very kind to me."

"Have you known her long?"

"Only a few weeks. It seems much longer than that."

"Where did you meet her?"

It did not seem in the least strange to Maeve that he should be curious. After all, they were all friends. And she had been interested to hear how Maud came to know Merton and glad, in a way, to know that it had been as her brother, Peter's, friend that he came to be at Saggart. With people as fundamentally pleasant as Maeve jealousy puts up such tiny shoots at first; they are hardly aware of its existence. Maeve asked Merton about the theatre and, of course, about theatrical personalities. Like most Irish people she had a yearning for drama.

"And what is Olivier like off the stage? Have you seen Alec Guinness in his new play? Do you think John Osborne is really important? Do you find Beckett exciting? Is Kenneth Tynan nice? How old is Harold Hobson?"

He answered all her questions. If a shade of malice might have been detected in his answers, it only added to the general gaiety of the conversation, and Maeve was unaware of it. In his turn he asked Maeve about the theatre in Dublin.

It was this which brought up the subject of the great charity performance for the rheumatism sufferers. Merton had heard of Mangan certainly, but grouped him in his mind with other Irish poets whose names cropped up occasionally but of whose work there seemed to be a regrettably hazy impression abroad.

"Yeats, of course, is a miracle. By far the greatest poet of the century. But about the others I must confess I don't know as much as I am sure I should."

Maeve told him of the dinner with Molly Pratt, the approach to Milton, the producer, the complicated scheme to arrange everything before the play was seen or the author consulted.

"It's the sort of situation that I would have called typically Irish," said Merton.

"You must not use that expression over here," said Maeve. "If we are critical we are also touchy."

It was when the car drew up at Saggart gate that Merton said lightly: "Is there any chance that I could get a part in that play? I am not acting in London this year. I have to go to Spain to make a film later on, but for the next two months I am on holiday. A weekend in Donegal will be quite enough. Could you use your influence with the casting director?"

"But you haven't seen the play."

"I know. I have become thoroughly Irish. You must have converted me."

* * *

The telephone rang for some time before Mangan answered it.

"Who is that?" His telephone manner suggested Faust in constant fear of a call from Mephistopheles.

"It's me."

"Oh, Molly."

"Were you ringing me up this afternoon, by any chance?"

"No. No. I didn't ring you up."

"I thought you might have. I wanted to say I was out this afternoon in case you rang up and wondered why you got no reply."

"Well, I didn't. But as you are there I might as well ask you : did I leave a brief-case with you? I have been searching everywhere."

"A black brief-case?"

"Yes. It's black."

"You did. I can see it now. That will give you some idea of how I've been neglecting the house lately. It was here just beside the telephone."

"I wish I had known. I've been wandering round half Dublin looking for it."

"You poor pet."

"I must get hold of it."

"Could you drop in this evening? I will be here. And I have something rather exciting to tell you. That was my principal reason for ringing up."

"What do you want to tell me?"

There was a note of scarcely suppressed irritation in Mangan's question. He disliked playful mysteries. If a person had something to say, let them say it (a principle which he did not always follow in literary composition). But, really, Molly seemed intent on wasting his time.

"It's about your play. I can't say more on the telephone."

"Why not? Why can't you say what you have to say on the telephone?"

"It's rather complicated. Come along as soon as you can. And I will have something nice for you. O.K.?"

"I'll be round in half an hour."

Mangan replaced the receiver slowly. There was no sign of elation in his manner. He suspected Molly of using some trivial pretext to get him to call on her. What could she know about his play? It was in London. And the people who had seen it in Dublin had refused to produce it. The woman was only trying to make herself important. And why had she not seen the brief-case? She must have known he left it. That was one decoy, the play was another. Now they had both been used. But she had not offered to deliver the brief-case. And much as he would have liked to, he had enough feeling for Molly not to have asked her to leave it somewhere to be collected. He had to walk into the trap. This was what he dreaded, this involvement.

Bridget put her head in the door.

"Did I hear the telephone?"

"I was talking on it."

"Nothing for me? I was expecting a call."

"No."

"I must run along. I left something for you in the oven. If Haggie rings up will you tell her to ring the office. It's a late night."

"I may be out myself. That was a call about my play. Evidently someone is interested in it."

"Good for you, Frank. Someone from the other side?"

"I think so. It's rather hush-hush at the moment. Don't say anything in the office. You know what this city is. Someone will try to cut in."

"I'll hold my tongue. I wish I'd known before I went to the trouble of making a meal. But the stew will keep. I must be off. I will say a prayer for you."

After Bridget left him, Mangan rose with an alacrity unusual for him and proceeded to change into a clean shirt and a pair of flannels that Bridget had recently pressed for him. He took trouble in selecting a tie.

"Do I need a shave?" he asked himself in the looking-glass.

He did. In the ordinary course he would have let the matter stand until tomorrow. But now, whatever had got into him, nothing would do him but to go through the tiresome rite. It refreshed him. He was glad, and thought what a pity it was one missed so much comfort in life by being too lazy to make an effort to attain it. He had not believed a word that Molly had said to him about the play, but he had been convinced by himself when he was making up that story for Bridget. It had the ring of truth about it.

He waited at the end of Marlborough Road for a bus into Dublin. Waiting for buses was a constant daily humiliation. Standing there while motor-cars streamed by was a constant reminder of one's failure. How ordinary, how common, how cheap and, indeed, how poor so many of these motorists looked as they went by; some very cautiously as if the effort to steer was a prodigious one; some casually; some in a mad rush as though escaping from crime. It was one of these rushing by that sent a shower of muddy water over Mangan and interrupted his morose reflections. For his heart had sunk again. He no longer believed his own story. And he cursed his weakness in taking Molly's bait.

It took her a very short time to put a match to the fire, settle the cushions and leave out cigarettes and glasses. But would she have time for a bath? Would it matter if Mangan came when she was having the bath? She played for a moment with an imaginary picture. Steam clouds and whiffs of bath salts in the air; a ring at the door; time only to grab a towel and push on slippers; then all radiant and rosy, rushing to the door—"Fix yourself a drink, darling"—back to the bathroom; door open, and chatter through the door; then the second appearance in a house-coat and slippers, feet still pink from the bath. It was a pleasing fantasy owing much to the skill of modern plumbing advertisements.

Unfortunately, Molly's bathroom was a builder's makeshift: and although she did her best, her efforts to lend it glamour were defeated by the geyser and the furniture of the room: the ceiling sloped inconveniently. Movement was frightfully restricted. And while she had often meant to treat herself to one of those large white comfortable turkish towels—when it came to the point economy prevailed. The towel she was using had tangerine stripes, and though perfectly clean, was skimpy. She tried to imagine the scene, so common in books, actually taking place here, with her own properties, and decided that at her age, and with Mangan's temperament, it had too many possibilities of anti-climax and indignity. Better just to change, powder and... God bless Harriet for that present of scent! She dabbed herself here and there. Behind the knees, she read somewhere, was a good place. She felt damn silly doing it.

She laughed at herself going to all this trouble, probably for no reason at all. But it gave confidence. Many an evening had been ruined by the nagging thought of a laddered stocking.

She was almost ready when the bell rang.

A little flustered, too anxious, perhaps, but genuinely happy because she had been so successful in her plans for him, Molly opened the door.

She did not expect Mangan to be fulsome. It would not be in character; but she was cast down to find him looking morose and suspicious. It threw her on the defensive, which was hardly fair when she was working for him. That it was her purpose to please him was beside the point. Who on this earth is completely kind and absolutely disinterested?

Mangan's first action on entering was to secure his brief-case. In the tiny flat it was hard to see how it could have lain undiscovered for ten minutes, and Molly did not refer to it again. She had, of course, seen it and seen him leave without it; but it had been so long since he had come to see her, it was tempting to keep this pledge to ensure an early return. He took no trouble to disguise the fact that it had served its purpose.

"That is the comfortable chair: or would you like the sofa? Let me give you a drink. This is a special brandy, a present, I need hardly say."

The chairs were small, so Mangan elected for the sofa. He nodded when Molly suggested a drink to signify assent. He was not talking because he was waiting to hear what Molly had to say. She did not rush into her topic because she wanted to get full value from the revelation, and, besides, she knew from experience that Mangan took some time to settle down. He had none of the social adaptability which is supposed to be an Irish attribute. The dourest Scot had nothing to teach him in the way of taciturnity.

"I lit the fire," said Molly as she sat on the rug and fanned her skirt out round her. "It seems absurd in July. But really it is so wet and cold I can't sit shivering at an empty grate just because the calendar says this is summer time. I do hope you didn't catch cold. I felt so sorry for you going out in those damp clothes. You did change when you got home, didn't you?"

Mangan nodded.

"Now I must make my confession." Molly looked down into her lap and pushed her skirts out with her hands like a little girl who has done something rather naughty. "You may be furious with me when I tell you."

And then she told him.

"Will they pay the usual royalties?" he said, after he had considered Molly's news.

"Of course. I mean—I took that for granted."

"Ah," Mangan gave an experienced and slightly patronising smile. "You can't afford to take things like that for granted. I know this crowd. They will be like all the others. All for notoriety and social humbug. But the artist must live on air. I have seen so much of it."

"But no one expects that. I don't certainly. I had only your interests at heart. I thought it might be an opportunity for you. I . . ." Molly fought back tears. "If you prefer to try something else, don't think of me. But I thought the other day you had been disappointed, that you felt neglected as all writers must who won't prostitute themselves to public taste. I'm sorry if I haven't pleased you."

Mangan was in fact both surprised and entirely satisfied with the scheme. The snags which he insisted on seeing were actually substitutes for the anxiety which was gnawing at his heart about the play itself. Blythe wrote a polite letter when he returned it from the Abbey. The radio people had excused themselves on account of its length. A new theatrical group with no fixed address to whom he had sent it finally—he tried to forget this—had neither acknowledged nor returned it. Unfortunately he had kept no record of posting it, and his threatening letters had been ignored with impunity. Fortunately he had a copy, but it was not encouraging. Nor was he convinced about the play's merits himself: it had been begun, abandoned, taken up again, put away, and finished in a scramble when he had spoken of it as a completed work and been invited to submit it to the Abbey. It lacked urgency. A wild scheme of re-writing entered Mangan's head for a moment and was as soon abandoned. I can always make improvements during rehearsal, he thought.

"God, how self-centred men are," thought Molly. "Why does one bother?"

Having considered every aspect of the matter save one, Mangan now thought of Molly's help. Since AE had encouraged him as a youth, no one had lifted a hand to help him.

"It was decent of you," he said.

Had he poured the riches of the East into her lap, Molly would not have valued it more than this reluctant, belated acknowledgement.

"Nonsense. Now we must stop worrying. There's a lot to do. But it can be done. Here, drink up. I don't want to be left with this bottle to nurse."

Mangan liked brandy.

They began to discuss questions of casting, production—a theatre had to be found.

"That reminds me. No one has seen the play yet. Would you bring it to me tomorrow—or post it."

"I've lost the second copy. The other is with the publisher."

"Aren't you the careless boy! losing a play at your age. How could you do it?"

Mangan did not want to be reminded of his frustrating and squalid experience with the local theatre group.

"I must have left it in a pub, I suppose. But I can write to the publisher. He is supposed to be reading it at the moment, but I don't suppose it will kill him to return it to be copied."

"Let me copy it. I have plenty of time at the moment. That ceramics job I told you about fell through."

"That's too bad." Mangan had forgotten.

The course which the evening was going to follow now depended upon him. Molly had told her story. The brief-case was restored. The brandy was finished. It was eight o'clock.

"I ought to be getting along," he said.

"Are you expected at home? I could toss up an omelette in no time—if that would be enough for you. And I have chutney. I know you like chutney. And there is the remains of a cheese cake. Does that tempt you?"

"What about your coming out and having a bite with me? It's not every night we pull off a deal like this one."

"I'm not dressed for that."

"Who is going to notice?"

Molly had in fact gone to some trouble with her clothes.

"I think we are much better here, unless you feel that you want something more substantial."

The debate might have become protracted, but the telephone halted it.

Molly kept the instrument beside her bed, and Mangan could not hear all that she was saying. But it had something to do with him and the play. He caught that. Something good: because Molly was shrieking delightedly. Other people's telephone conversations always seem to be interminable. This was no exception. Mangan began to feel a grievance. But the conversation came to an end at last.

Molly came back into the room, her small eyes shining, her arms out-stretched.

"Frank, darling. I can hardly believe it. Merton Sandys wants to act in the play. For nothing! I swear it. That was Maeve O'Connell. He *asked* for a part. Oh, my darling, I am so glad for you."

"I'm not sure that he will make much of it. I'm not impressed by the West-End-type actor. It's about time we realised that we have talent every bit as good ourselves. Why can't we take our eyes off London?"

There's no pleasing him, Molly thought. But he did relax, if grudgingly, and again suggested taking her out to dinner.

A few minutes earlier she had wanted to go out, but waited to be persuaded as she knew Mangan was not given to deeds of hospitality. But now she would have preferred to stay. His softened mood had possibilities. And it was months since he had even bothered to kiss her. But Mangan knew himself in certain essential respects, and he knew that he could only ensure the success of the evening, if at inconvenient expense, by going out. To stay here, for the sake of a few pounds, was to court disaster of one kind or another.

CHAPTER IX

A LARGE, FRECKLE-FACED BOY who seemed recently to have outgrown the sports-clothes he was wearing, stood uncomfortably in the lobby of the National Gallery. He glanced at his watch from time to time and between the intervals looked cautiously around him. Nothing caught his attention save a portrait of Parnell which glared at him as thought demanding an explanation of his visit. Unable to withstand this scrutiny the boy glanced cautiously through the door on his left and saw a large nude which, having looked around to make sure he was alone, he examined more carefully. Was she, the boy wondered, a professional model? Or, perhaps, an artist's wife? Or did they do these things without models? And if you were an artist could you ask girls to pose for you? It all presented to his imagination a notion of a world so entirely different from his own, and so entirely different from the years that lay ahead in the office of a chartered accountant.

"I hope I haven't kept you waiting."

The young man, interrupted in his reverie, was blushing when he turned to face Maeve O'Connell. She had been running and her face was flushed for that reason.

"It was nice of you to come, Gerry," she said. "I was awfully anxious to talk to you."

"But why here?"

"I wanted to be sure we would be alone. Come into this room where the Irish pictures are. There's nowhere to sit down but we can pretend to be looking at *Cattle at Malahide*. Do you come here often?"

"No. This is the first time I've been here. I often meant to come."

"I want to talk to you about Johnny. Look at this." Maeve looked around, as her companion had, a few minutes earlier, to see if she was being observed before handing him a sheet of newspaper which she took out of her bag.

"You see that." She pointed to a headline:

ANOTHER BORDER RAID. HUTS AT FRONTIER POSTS BLOWN UP.

The young man looked uncomfortable.

"It looks like one of the usual raids," he said. "I don't see anything very remarkable about it."

"Johnny has been away for two days. He said he was staying with you. How long has he been mixed up in this?"

"Johnny doesn't tell me what he does."

"But you know he is in the I.R.A."

"Look here, Maeve. What are you getting at? I was a friend of Sean's, but that doesn't mean I am his nurse. And it certainly does not mean I am going to talk about him behind his back, even to his family."

"But someone must get him to see sense. It's such a crazy business. And sooner or later someone's going to be killed."

"Some have been."

"I know. I meant that Johnny would be implicated in a killing. I would hate him if I heard he had blown someone up in a booby-trap. And I don't want him to be shot either. And either way it's such a waste of his life. He has changed so much. We used to have great fun. Now he is like a ghoul."

"I don't see much of him lately."

"You were his best friend. Surely you could talk to him. Tell him I was on to you, if you like. He knows I suspect him. I as much as told him so."

Gerry in his awkward way admired Maeve, and would have been glad enough to make himself pleasing to her. He had been quite at a loss to understand why she had wanted to see him, had even faintly hoped that it might be for some reason favourable to him. He had expected no possibility so depressing as this. Gerry was a country boy, and in his blood was the old horror of informing. It was the sin of Judas to report anyone, however horrible their crime. Gerry would have talked quite freely about his suspicions, John was open about his politics; but once a specific act had taken place which involved the police, then it was another matter.

"I want to keep my father and mother out of this. But they

are bound to know sooner or later. Where could I see Johnny? Do you think he is on the far side of the Border?"

"Honestly, Maeve, there is no use in asking me."

"But he may want help."

"If you promise not to mention my name, I can tell you someone who might be able to put you right. But you will want to be pretty tactful. Do you know Tony Kelly?"

"I never heard of him."

"He lives in a house near the Silver Fox Farm at Enniskerry. I think people called Tone own it. If you could find him and say you want to help, he might do something. But I'm afraid he will have to be convinced that you are breast high with Sean in the cause before he will let you in on anything."

"If he asks me how I heard of him what shall I say?"

Gerry pondered.

"Don't say Sean told you. And don't say I told you. I tell you what: say you were looking for Sean round college and you met someone who said he might know. Say it was a girl that you had never seen before, with red hair and a northern accent. But don't say I told you, mind."

Some people had come into the gallery. Maeve heard voices behind her and thrust the paper back into her bag. It did not matter now. At least she had a clue and could do something. But she blushed guiltily when she saw Maud and Merton Sandys coming across the room. Gerry's habitual gaucherie did not help him to carry off the situation. He felt ill at ease in these surroundings, and Maud's manner did nothing to lessen his sense of inadequacy. Maeve was anxious not to give a false impression. But what impression was she to give? She saw Merton look at her kindly but curiously. Maud, without appearing to do so, was taking stock of Gerry. There was something in Maud's glance that seemed to test and find wanting anything she looked at for the first time. This was very apparent in her survey of Gerry's general appearance. For his part the afternoon had gone from bad to worse, and now he only wanted to get away. But, like Maeve, he felt the necessity of giving some cover to their encounter. Unlike Maeve he was indifferent to what form that cover took. And Maeve was torn between the claims of secrecy, her anxiety not to give Merton a wrong impression, and an uncomplicated distaste which she knew was mean and shameful, for being discovered with such an uncouth acquaintance.

"It's extraordinary to meet three people one knows in here," said Maeve. "I am usually on my own."

"I want to show Merton the Goyas," said Maud. "I think they are round the corner somewhere. Do you," she said, turning to Gerry, "like Goya as much as I do? I'd give all this (they were passing through the Dutch room now) for a Goya."

She could talk of nothing but Goya and bustled Merton along when he stopped to look at a small Rembrandt that had caught his eye.

"Rembrandt is too solemn. Frightfully Protestant, don't you think? I am sure Goya practised black magic."

"You know what I mean," she appealed to Gerry. "Merton is such a prig. He thinks Goya is too worldly for his taste. Look at him. What did I tell you?"

She flashed a brilliant smile at Gerry, curling him up with embarrassment.

They had arrived at the Goyas, but Merton, instead of looking at them, had turned to a large St Francis by El Greco on the opposite wall.

"Goya is Maud's latest discovery, as you may have noticed," he said to Maeve, doggedly refusing to put himself in position for a lecture.

"We much prefer this, don't we?" said Maud to Gerry who, sweating now, followed her glance towards a painting of an entrancing gipsy with a black mop of hair and a pouting mouth. Nothing could have provided a greater contrast to the ecstasies of the emaciated saint.

Gerry had no idea what to say. He felt miserably ill at ease. Maud's pretence of enlisting him on her side made him more uncomfortable—because it seemed to require an effort from him —than if she had left him alone.

"It comes from visiting galleries with one's governess. Merton has never recovered from that. He associates pictures with lessons and nursery tea. He wallows in gloom. Come and I will show you my favourite picture here."

Merton did not want to follow Maud, whom he found tiresome in this mood. Maeve would have been delighted to stay with him; but she was sure that Maud wanted to make mischief, and she was unhappy at the thought of the wretched Gerry who had the despairing look of a non-swimmer caught in a current. She would have to rescue him.

She did not know how to say this to Merton, but when she looked at him she felt that he understood and that no explanations were necessary. She felt suddenly grateful to him. It was so difficult, as a rule, even to communicate with words; what a relief to find someone who knew instinctively what one thought.

They followed the others. Maud small, but upright and authoritative in her walk, looking now like a band leader. Gerry slouched behind her trying, apparently, to find cover by wriggling his head and neck backwards through his shirt collar.

Maud took her stand before a large picture in the main gallery. Two girls, apparently on a picnic, are looking away; one in grey sits with her back turned, holding a sunshade which is going to prove inadequate against the huge black cloud massing in the sky. But she seems unperturbed by this, as does her companion, who looks serene and beautiful. The rain will hardly dare to fall on her. In the foreground a rustic, a boy in peasant's dress, faces the spectator and points enigmatically at the girls, a few inches away in space, but divided by a world between them. On the left, in shadow, a pretty girl lies on the ground looking up at the boy. A cow's head looks into the picture on the right.

"Isn't that delightful," Maud began. "Italian decadence, of course. Tiepolo never seems really to *believe* in what he is doing. But I love it."

The others stared, stunned by Maud's patter or resentful at the way she had taken over since she came into the gallery.

"It's wonderfully romantic," Maeve said. "But posed, don't you feel? Not something seen."

"That's it's chief charm," Maud replied pat. "It's so wonderfully untrue to life. The cow now. He has never been milked."

"I hope not," said Merton gently. "She is, perhaps, a bull."

But Maud, oddly excited, did not notice the confusion.

"The only earthly thing is the girl in the foreground. He was probably in love with her."

"The cow?"

"Tiepolo, the artist. He puts a positive glow on her. The other women are so detached and picturesque and untouchable."

Gerry who had been reading the label on the picture in sheer desperation became more confused than ever.

"It says here that the picture is by Piazzetta," he said.

Maud took a quick step forward, read, and frowned.

"Of course. How silly of me. He was Tiepolo's son-in-law."

"I can see a great advantage in modern painting," Merton murmured. "All these confusions of sex and mistaken identities are eliminated. There is a lot to be said for Liberty Hall."

"I must be going, Maeve," said Gerry piteously. He had stayed long enough, he thought, to give an appearance of verisimilitude to her story, but every moment of this sort of conversation made him feel more desperate, and he had conceived a horror of Maud who seemed determined to expose his ignorance.

"It was nice to meet you, Gerry," said Maeve.

"Remember me to Sean."

He nodded brusquely at Merton, and shyly at Maud, then walked with an awkward but determined stride across the gallery and down the staircase. He felt that his back was under surveillance, and was tempted to run.

But in fact Maud had returned to the picture and continued the discussion.

Maeve tried to catch Merton's eye. For the first time since she had known her she found herself critical of Maud. Why was she going on like this? Whom was she seeking to impress?

"What time is your hair appointment?" said Merton.

Maud looked at her watch. "Heavens. I'm late. It won't take more than three minutes in the car. Where will I meet you, Merton?"

He hesitated. "Your hair do will take an hour or so. I am going to take Maeve off to tea at the Russell: will you come along and join us there?"

"Splendid," said Maud. But she did not look pleased.

She did not look at Maeve, and hurried away, raising one hand in valediction to them both.

Without Maud, whose tone had been so didactic, and the disorientated Gerry, Maeve found herself enjoying the gallery. Merton had knowledge and a light touch. It was this which appealed to her more than anything else about him. What he liked about her was her freedom from cliché. None of the women with whom he could have imagined himself visiting a gallery would have had to consider their opinion before any picture. Instinct would have said it was 'in' or 'out' just as certainly as it would have directed their choice of clothes. It was much worse to be boringly right than amusingly wrong. Merton's wife had been very 'amusing'. She believed in nothing and lived in dread of everything. Her life was lived behind masks. That they were masks in the best of taste did not make them more real.

Walking across St Stephen's Green they discussed the play. Maeve had broken the news of Merton's desire to act to her mother as well as to Molly Pratt. Theatre managers were being interviewed. Dates were being arranged.

"It would be nice," said Merton, "to see the play. Are we sure there is a male cast? There is something very mysterious about that part of the venture. Authors, as a rule, push their scripts at one. This diffidence is something new in my experience."

"Mrs Pratt is our only source of information. She keeps the author locked up in a cupboard somewhere. I must say she has been pretty vague. However, it's promised by the time you come back from Donegal next week."

In the hotel Maeve seemed so preoccupied that at last Merton asked her what was the matter. "Were we untactful this afternoon, blundering in like that? Your friend was frightened of Maud. I could see that. I don't altogether blame him. You didn't look very pleased to see us. I felt quite jealous."

"I was embarrassed and I told a lie. I had not met Gerry by accident."

"That was obvious to everybody."

"Oh!"

"You are not the conspiratorial type. Nor, indeed, is he."

"But you must not get a wrong impression. Gerry was a school friend of my brother's. I am worried about my brother at the moment."

"I know that. I wish I could help."

"If I tell you something, will you promise not to repeat it to Maud or anyone."

"I promise."

"Swear."

"I swear."

And for the second time in the course of a week Maeve gave

her confidence. Merton did not receive it flippantly as Maud had done, but he did not share Maeve's sense of doom. "Is it the danger he is in that upsets you?"

"Partly. But more the feeling of surprise that someone so close to me could be involved in it. The I.R.A. is something like death or crime, something that happens to other people, something outside oneself."

"It's your bourgeois instincts that are violated. Your brother is not being respectable—isn't that it?"

"My parents will feel that. Perhaps I do—a little. One doesn't think of oneself that way. I am awfully bourgeois, I suppose. But leaving my brother out of it, I think these Border raids are stupid. I think they are wrong. I hate violence and arrogance. Why should a small group of people take it on themselves to wage a war? If innocent people are killed by my brother I shall hate him for it. I know that."

"What can we do?"

"I believe Johnny was in the raid yesterday. He is so much away from home my parents have ceased to notice it. They believe he is staying with friends and swotting for exams. Neither has the least idea of what university life is. Mother won't hear anything against Johnny. And my father is one of those people who avoid trouble until it hits them. I have a feeling that Johnny is in trouble at the moment. If he got away, he should have turned up today."

"He is probably in hiding."

"But that means he is on the far side of the Border. I am sure he was meant to get back after the raid."

"You must wait."

"I can't. My only chance is to find Johnny now. If I do that I might be able to reason with him. At home it is impossible. He thinks of himself as a lone idealist surrounded by traitors to the cause. It was bad enough when he had his religious phase: but it was nothing in comparison to this."

"I think you would be very foolish to mix yourself up in this affair. There are probably some fairly grim characters at the back of it. If you think of the risks they are running they can't afford to take a kindly view of some girl who comes poking her nose into their business. And you ought to think of your brother's position. If he becomes a liability on your account, it may be dangerous for him."

"I can't take them seriously. They are little boys playing Cops and Robbers. It's the dullness of life in Ireland. Old men drink and young ones blow up statues. What is the alternative? Everyone is not religious. And very few people get a kick out of talking to themselves in Irish. But there has been no other solution offered. We are incapable of the day-to-day effort the English make. We must do something desperate if we do anything at all. It's quite incredible how a few fanatics get their way in everything. No one else cares enough to make an effort."

"The best lack all conviction while the worst
Are full of passionate intensity," he murmured.

"Who said that?"

"Your arrogant, great poet, Yeats."

"It's awfully true."

"And the women—what do they do?"

"The women do the washing-up."

"Poor women."

The apparition of Maud cut the conversation short. An understanding seemed to have become established between Maeve and Merton. It was not necessary to enjoin silence or to arrange for a new meeting. These things would be. But Maeve had taken a resolve which she was going to disclose to nobody, not to Maud, whose spell had been broken; nor to Merton, because he was English and looked at Ireland with friendly but foreign eyes. She refused Maud's invitation to dinner and slipped away.

* * *

A muddy cart-track between brambles which scratched the bonnet of the car as if resenting an intruder ended with a five-bar iron gate which swayed on its hinges with a dismal creak. The car squeezed through the attenuated entrance into a yard which was flanked by decrepit stables roofed with corrugated iron. A few thin hens rushed out of the gate clucking, flapping their moulting wings, the only living things to be seen. Rain and manure made brown puddles in which lay debris of various kinds—old car tyres, iron bedsteads, old boots, tins and a bowler hat. One stable had a door and this was locked.

Maeve had been directed to this derelict spot in her search for the Tone farm. She was beginning to think there was a mistake. Then, standing at a door in the corner of the yard which she had overlooked, she saw a girl. At the apparition Maeve became nervous about the wisdom of this expedition upon which she had embarked so impulsively. The girl was dark and thick-set, a farm girl. Her expression was not hostile but ruminative; she was not going to take the initiative. Maeve abandoned the car and picked her way through the puddles.

"Is this Mr Tone's house?" she asked.

"Which of them is it you are looking for?" said the girl.

"I want to see Mr Tony Kelly. I believe he lives here."

The girl made no reply to this but turned and went indoors. After a while she returned.

"Who is it that wants him?" she said.

"My name is Maeve O'Connell. He knows my brother."

"I'll see if he is in the house," said the girl, and disappeared again.

A very ragged child came to the door, stared hard at Maeve, and then ran indoors again. After a further delay a heavy, middle-aged man in a dirty flannel shirt and very old stained tweed trousers came to the door. He held it half-closed as though expecting Maeve to rush it.

"Who are you looking for?" he said.

"Mr Tony Kelly. He is a friend of my brother's. I want to see him."

"He doesn't live here," said the man.

The lie lay heavy on the air; Maeve, loth to admit defeat, found herself scrutinising the suspicious man who, in turn, stared at her. It was some time before she spoke.

"Can you tell me where I can find him then? It's most important."

"Who did you say you were?"

"Maeve O'Connell is my name."

"Wait there a minute." The man went indoors again.

"Have you a message for Tony Kelly?" he said when he returned. "I will be seeing him maybe. And I can tell him whatever it is you want to know."

"I must see himself. It's about my brother. Where can I find Mr Kelly?"

"Wait there."

Once more the man went in. He came back very promptly this time.

"Step in," he said.

The door was very low. It lead into a flagged kitchen. The interior was almost as deserted-looking as the yard. An old range, rusting in the corner, had not been used for many years. There were a few kitchen chairs, a deal cupboard and against the side wall a table at which someone had been recently having a cup of tea. The girl who had seen Maeve come into the yard stood in a corner holding the child against her skirt. They stared at Maeve, the child curiously, the young woman with the same bucolic stare. The man opened an inner door and nodded to Maeve to go through it. Then he fastened the door and left her alone with a man who had been sleeping in his clothes on an iron bed in the corner, but now sat on the edge of it and stared at Maeve through thick spectacles.

He was unshaven, and there were flecks of grey in his red beard. His hair which stood upright and which he wore cut close was also turning grey. His face was gnarled and could have never been young. He could have been forty, but was probably nearer to fifty. His clothes reminded Maeve of Johnny's. The Parker pen which he wore in his breast pocket, the Oxford Dictionary on the table beside a Penguin copy of Joyce's *Dubliners*, were not in keeping with the general appearance of a farm labourer.

He said nothing but continued to keep Maeve under a close scrutiny as if she were a specimen under a microscope. There was a chair in the room on which she sat down. And as Mr Kelly continued to keep silent she took out her cigarette case and offered him one. He nodded refusal.

"Do you mind if I do?"

He nodded again as if impatient with her irrelevance.

"You wanted to see me," he said at last.

"I'm sorry for tracking you down like this. But it's about my brother, John. I am worried about him. I thought you might be able to help."

"What makes you think that?"

His voice was cold; his accent slightly artificial. He sounded like a schoolmaster.

"I thought you . . . I heard that you were a friend of Johnny's and were likely to know his movements."

"Did Johnny, as you call him, tell you that?"

"I never heard Johnny mention your name."

"Then who told you?"

"Someone I saw when I was looking for Johnny round college. Someone I had never seen before."

"A man?"

"Not exactly."

"What do you mean?"

"I was talking to a group of people and someone—I think it was a girl—said you were a person who might know."

"And where was this group?"

"In college. At the University. I was looking for Johnny. He has not been home for several days."

"But this is not term time. How did you find a group in college. Do you mean at Earlsfort Terrace?"

"That is where the College is. Where else could I mean?"

"I can't tell you, Miss O'Connell."

He knows I have been lying, thought Maeve, I should have taken more trouble. Her attitude towards the secret forces of the revolutionaries had been so contemptuous that she had not reckoned with the fact that she might have someone formidable to deal with.

"The person who told me did so under a promise of secrecy. I have no interest in your organisation. I am only concerned for my brother. I believe him to be in danger, and I want to help him if I can."

"What sort of danger, Miss O'Connell?"

"He hasn't come home. He must be in hiding. I want to get him to this side of the Border."

"And what makes you think he is on the other side?"

"The fact that he didn't come home after it."

"After what?"

"The raid."

"I don't know what you are talking about."

"I can't believe that, Mr Kelly."

"I am sorry. I advise you to go home. I also advise you to be careful what you say. The government of this so-called Republic has the democratic practice of locking-up without trial those whom it suspects of being engaged in armed combat with the British forces occupying the six counties. If it came to the ears of the government that Sean O'Connell's sister was talking in this way, he might find himself behind bars at the Curragh. I am sure you don't want that to happen."

He took off his thick spectacles. It should have humanised him. So long as he kept them on Maeve felt as if she was listening to a voice issuing from behind a grille. So far from decreasing his aloofness, the result of this gesture was to make the thought of contact on any human level quite hopeless. The eyes behind the spectacles did not look myopic. There is something pathetic in blindness. They were pale and expressionless, or it might be more accurate to say—fixed in one expression, not altogether cold (although it was cold) or harsh (it was steely enough) but something that combined these and yet suggested a third, a remote and indefinable quality. They were the eyes of a madman. And Maeve felt suddenly afraid.

"I have not told anyone about Johnny."

"You told me: and you told a group of students who assembled for the purpose, apparently, although it is holiday time."

"I was trying to cover up. I don't want to give away the person who told me to ask you."

"I shall find him soon enough."

"You assume it is a 'he'."

"Sean . . ." Kelly began. And then he hesitated. It was the first glimpse of human feeling he had shown. He could change his mind.

"Johnny doesn't have girl friends," Maeve finished the sentence for him. "But that doesn't prevent girls from taking an interest in him."

She left it at that. And she got the impression from Kelly's silence that he believed her. He changed the subject:

"Have you thought about my position? You come up here making enquiries. You bandy my name about and, no doubt, describe me as a member of the organisation. I can be arrested and imprisoned without trial. If you combine the charge against me with an admission about your brother, that will be good enough for both of us. You are a dangerous acquaintance."

"This is nonsense. If I wanted to make trouble I had only

to tell my parents or the college authorities. But I want nothing of the kind. I am anxious about my brother. My instinct tells me he is in danger and I want to help him."

"And you proceed to discuss his affairs with anyone and everyone."

"I do nothing of the kind."

"Who do you think I am? What do you know about me? Suppose I go down to the police and report our conversation. What then?"

"That is silly."

"Who am I then?"

"A friend of Johnny's. That is all I know."

"Are you prepared to talk like this to all Johnny's friends?"

"Have it your own way. I took a chance when I spoke to you like this. I see that. But if you will forgive me, there is something about the set-up here that suggests a conspiracy of some kind."

"And what is that, may I ask?"

"Getting to see you. When I call on someone as a rule, I'm not screened as I was this evening. If the police did come they would have enough to confirm their suspicions before they even met you."

"I was asleep. My friend did not want to disturb me. It is rather late for a lady to pay calls, you know. Did it occur to you that a simple countryman might have been on his guard against a strange woman who clamours to see a man at this hour? You are not used to country ways. I like it here. I can read and I am not interrupted. I like my privacy, Miss O'Connell. My friend knows that."

Maeve wished she had not spoken, but her confidence began to return. Kelly had no idea whether she had mentioned this visit to anyone in Dublin. Her car had been seen in the neighbourhood. He was keeping up this bluff of being a harmless citizen which any show of violence would call immediately. But, on the other hand, how was he to let her go? If she went back to Dublin frustrated by the visit, more anxious than ever about her brother, she was more than likely to repeat what had happened. Maeve and Kelly were thinking this together, as she knew when he spoke.

"I am worried for my own sake. You don't seem to be

discreet. You will talk when you get back to Dublin, and before I know anything, the guards will have taken me into custody. I can't allow that."

"Why not accept my offer? If I help to rescue Johnny I shall be as guilty in the eyes of the law as he is. You will be much better off letting me into the secret than keeping me out of it."

"There is no secret."

"What is the use of this humbug? I was a fool to come here. I see that. But you are showing a great lack of imagination in not taking my offer."

"You get your ideas from the cinema, Miss O'Connell."

"I assumed I was talking to someone with ideas." She glanced at the books on the window sill and on the chair beside the bed. "If you were just a thug I would not have suggested it."

"I suppose you think most of the people who are prepared to fight for your freedom are thugs."

Maeve recognised the tone of voice. It was Johnny's and her father's when he recalled historical grievances—the tune to which a hymn of hate had been set and which endless repetition had made mechanical.

"You sound like Johnny when you say that," she said.

Kelly, aware that he had let down his defences for a moment, made no answer to this. The gleam that had momentarily brought life into his pale eyes went as quickly as it came. It was almost as though a light had been switched off, precaution against enemy attack. But Maeve had no time to ponder this: her attention was riveted by the sound of a motor-car in the yard. Kelly sat up at this—he had been lying back against the wall—and glanced at his watch. He seemed to consider for a moment, then he said:

"I must leave you for a few minutes. I'll be back."

He went out, shutting the door firmly behind him. A moment's hesitation outside the door before his feet sounded on the kitchen flags suggested that he had toyed with the idea of locking it.

He did not come back for half an hour. It seemed many times longer than that to Maeve who found her chair hard but thought it better not to move lest Kelly, for whom suspicion had become an occupational disease, should suspect her of prying. She picked up a copy of *Dr Zhivago* which lay within reach, but found she could not concentrate. It seemed quite incoherent, a jumble of names and disconnected sentences. In the distance she could hear voices, sometimes low, sometimes raised. Her fate, she had no doubt, was being decided.

Then Kelly came back. He stood against the window, a squat indistinguishable shape were it not for the strange round head unmistakable even in shadow.

"I have heard that Sean is in the north. He wants to get away, but his plans have miscarried. If you will go to a place which you will be told later, at a time we can arrange, he will get into your car and you can bring him across the Border. The objection to this is the fact that your car will be noticed going up with no passenger and returning with one. It is very important that Sean should get back. I must give the matter more thought. But you are not to consult anyone. Do you get that?"

"Are you asking me to swear?"

"Oaths have gone out of fashion here. They got a bad name. I will say only this: if you don't keep your mouth shut your brother may go to prison for ten years. The Northern judges are not free from political prejudice. You can never be quite certain who is checking up on your confidences. Soldiers do not usually have an enemy at home as well as abroad to contend with. But that is the position of Sean's organisation. So it keeps its mouth shut and its eyes and ears open."

"When shall I go?"

"We can decide that later."

"How will I get in touch with you?"

"Don't worry. We will make contact."

She saw a small car in the yard, a Volkswagen probably. But there was no one about in the yard or in the kitchen. Kelly stood in the door and watched her until she started up the engine. She turned to wave at him. But the door had shut and the house was in darkness.

CHAPTER X

"OH, MISS TUFFY."

"Yes, Sir Walter."

"Here is a letter from Francis Xavier Mangan, he wants a loan of the manuscript he left with us."

"Mangan?"

"Yes, you know, the Irish poet."

"But I have no manuscript of his."

"Nonsense, Miss Tuffy. Don't you remember? I gave him an advance, a crazy advance; but he got the soft side of me."

"I remember the cheque. I brought it in and you gave it to him. One hundred pounds. That was about a week ago. But I never saw a manuscript."

"Think again. I meant to ask you to let me see it; but, to be quite frank, until it is acted somewhere, I can't see a play of his selling a hundred copies."

"You must have taken it yourself, Sir Walter."

"I don't keep a dog, Miss Tuffy, and bark myself. Go and have a look to put my mind at rest."

Miss Tuffy left in what her employer called 'one of her humours'. He began to calculate her probable age. She came the year the war ended. That September. She had been someone's secretary before the war for a bit. In her middle forties. She didn't look it. If she were going to be difficult it would be much better if she took herself off and was difficult somewhere else. Women. Women. Women. Always having to be humoured. Sweetness itself, all ears, until they felt themselves secure. Then nag, nag, nag. Or, worse, martyrdom. Miss Tuffy was the martyr type. 'Oh, it's nothing. Just a headache. It will go during the day.' A young person, new to the job, enthusiastic, ambitious; with some life outside the office. That would be refreshing for a change. But he would never have the heart to do it.

"Oh, Miss Tuffy."

She had returned looking dour and determined.

"There is no manuscript," she said.

"But he says he left it here. I distinctly remember a rather disgusting brown paper parcel. Don't you remember?"

"No, Sir Walter."

"But this is very serious."

"I can't help it, Sir Walter."

"What am I going to do, Miss Tuffy?"

"Write and ask him if he took it away."

"But he says distinctly that he left it here. He wants it back because he has no other copy. Someone is going to put the play on for him in Dublin. That is why he is in a hurry."

"Why did he not keep a copy? Everyone keeps a carbon copy of their manuscript."

"He probably lost it. Or he didn't have one. Most of it is in handwriting. He is Irish, you know."

"He ought to have a second copy."

"Really, Miss Tuffy. What use is it to stand there and say he ought to have a second copy? What am I going to do? He will threaten to sue me for damages. God, what a fool I am. Why did I give him an advance? I knew I should never see a penny of it again, Miss Tuffy."

But Miss Tuffy was unrelenting. Any sign of weakness on her part would, she knew, be taken down and used as evidence against her.

"We can't waste all day over him. Come. Take a letter."

He leaned back in his chair. Miss Tuffy sat down and put her notebook on the desk.

Dear Francis Xavier Mangan,

I am delighted to hear that the play is going to be produced. You will remember I suggested that a performance would greatly help sales by whetting public interest in the work. I wish you every success.

Have you not got a second copy? I would return the one that you say you left here with pleasure, but, unfortunately, it has gone to a reader. I looked at it myself, of course, but I felt that it would be better to have the views of an outside reader. I can not take an impartial view, as you know, of any of your work. I am hopelessly prejudiced in its favour. I can only hope that our reader will confirm the favourable impression I received from a quick reading.

Ever yours,

"That will keep him quiet for a bit."

Sir Walter always felt better after dictating. It had a cathartic effect.

Miss Tuffy checked her notes.

"*Say you left here?* Doesn't that suggest a doubt?"

"But there is a doubt, isn't there?"

"Not when you go on to say you sent it to a reader."

"Quite so. It must be one thing or the other. Make any change you like. The important thing is to get a letter off to him. And you will keep an eye out for the manuscript, won't you?"

"I put manuscripts into a file under the author's name until they go to the reader. I am positive Mr Mangan's was not given to me."

Tears welled up in Miss Tuffy's eyes. Tears against injustice. Tears of neglect. Tears of wasted devotion.

"Yes, of course. I was only speaking in a most general way. It can't do any harm to keep an eye out. That is all I meant to say. Thank you, Miss Tuffy."

She rushed from the room.

There was no doubt about it. Life is difficult enough, he thought, without this. It will go on for a year. Perhaps longer. What a beginning to a day!

* * *

Tomorrow, Friday, Merton was leaving for Donegal. He would come back on Monday or Tuesday.

Maeve heard this on the telephone very late on Thursday night. She rang Maud up when she got back from her interview with Tony Kelly to make an unconvincing apology for having left the Russell so abruptly. It was a quite unnecessary call which a week before would have been the most natural gesture in the world. The girls had got into the way of ringing one another up on the slightest pretext. Since Merton had arrived there had been a change; how great a change Maeve only realised when Maud answered the telephone and it was necessary to say something. Spontaneity had gone. And yet Maud sounded the same. When she said: "Merton is here. Would you like to say something to him?" it seemed quite unforced. "You say it for me. I must go to bed," Maeve replied, realising that when she rang up Maud, she was in fact ringing up Merton. She was thankful for the meagre satisfaction of knowing that he at least was there. "Hold on," said Maud. And Merton came to the telephone. The sound of his voice caused Maeve always a slight falling in the pit of her stomach. And she had to sit down. She had to concentrate hard to prevent herself from talking too fast.

He told her his weekend plans. When he came back he was staying at Saggart until Horse Show week was over. Then he would stay in an hotel unless he could find a flat for himself. Could Maeve find him a flat? It was pleasanter to have one's own place. He supposed a temporary servant could be picked up.

When Maeve put the telephone down, she was surprised to find that she had been talking for half an hour. It was one o'clock.

During the night—she slept very little—she hatched a plan. If she drove Merton up to Donegal, Johnny could be picked up somewhere and driven back. Merton would return by train. If there was a close inspection of traffic on the border, this would get over the difficulty. Merton would probably be glad of the lift. It would give her confidence to have his company.

The idea was so attractive that she went back to Wicklow immediately after breakfast. The Tone farm had the same deserted air as on the previous evening. But this time, even when she banged on the door with her fists, there was no answer. The Volkswagen was no longer in the yard. The stable door that had been locked now creaked on its hinges. Even the hens had gone. She felt frightened for the second time since the adventure began.

When she got home she rang Merton up. A servant answered the telephone. Maeve was relieved that she was not to have Maud as an intermediary.

"Is that you, Merton? How are you travelling today?"

"I meant to go by train this afternoon, but now they want me to lunch in Enniskillen tomorrow and drive from there. It's rather a bore."

"Could I drive you?"

"That would be divine, but absurd unless you could stay for the weekend. Why not? I can ask Mossy if he has room for another guest. I am sure he has in that barrack of his."

"I can't do that. I have to look someone up. But it would suit me splendidly to drive you to Enniskillen if you can arrange transport from there."

"Has this anything to do with our recent conversation? Who are you looking up? Is it—?"

"Prenez garde."

"If it's your relation who has an infectious complaint, I am not going to help you to catch it."

"I can explain that when I see you. I must get busy with the Customs if we are to be off in the morning. I shall call immediately after breakfast."

"I have a good mind to say 'no'."

"We can talk about that tomorrow."

When Maeve put down the telephone, her mother came in bustling with excitement.

"Was that for me?" she said.

"No."

"Who was it?" Kate did not encourage reticence.

"Merton Sandys."

"I wish I had known. Maureen MacLaverty is bothering the life out of me about him. I must say your friend Maud has worked a miracle in collecting him for us. I think he must be sweet on her. What do you think?"

"I have seen no sign of it."

"Why don't you bring him along and let us all meet him. I am dying to see what he's like."

"He is going away for the weekend."

"Do you think he would be back on Wednesday? I want to throw a cocktail party for him."

"Oh, Mummy."

"What's wrong with that? Why do you want to throw cold water on everything? Everyone is dying to meet him. And we can get a load of hospitality off our chest. It will be a chance to introduce him to the committee. And I think we ought to have the theatre management here. Will he expect champagne? I don't think your daddy would take too kindly to the idea of putting it up for that number. We might compromise by having a few bottles in reserve until the end of the party. Will you sit down this afternoon and write the invitations with me?"

"I hate cocktail parties. And I don't believe Merton will want to meet a whole crowd of strangers. Until the play turns up nothing can be decided anyway."

"It's a wonder how we all managed to live before you were born, miss. Actors love a crowd. There's nothing you can tell me about actors. Thank you."

"But Merton—Mr Sandys—is not like that. You would never know he was an actor. He has come here for a rest."

"And he takes the first part that he hears of. Come off it, child. Just because he knows your precious Maud doesn't mean that he shares her stick-in-the-mud attitude. He is making use of her, of course. They always do. Spongers the whole lot of them. In my father's place on a Sunday there used to be open house, and you should have seen how much the theatrical crowd put away. It doesn't matter what they earn, they never have the price of a box of matches on them. And they never refuse a square meal. Don't tell me about actors."

"But you haven't met him, Mummy. To begin with he is very successful and famous. I can't see that the sort of people we will introduce him to can do him any good. I mean—it will be much more interesting for them to meet him than for him to meet them."

"And do you want to keep him for yourself? Is that your idea? You are very selfish in some ways, Maeve."

"I regard him as someone whom I met in a friend's house and whom I happen to like. Surely that is better than to look on him as a sort of cake one is greedy not to share."

"Soon we will have to be careful if you deign to come among us. Ever since you met this Mountstephen woman you have become so *graund* we can't hope to live up to you."

"I don't feel like cocktail parties, Mummy. And he is my friend. Why should I have no say in the matter?"

"I suppose he is married. A few times, I expect." Kate was shifting her ground.

Maeve hesitated. Her mother was in such a combative mood that she had to think over each remark now as if she were in the boxing ring and might by carelessness leave herself exposed to a knockout blow. Kate was quite capable of falling back on her rights as guardian of her daughter's morals if she could not gain her objective any other way. Maeve did not like lying: but her mother's assaults had taught her to feint. She feinted now.

"What has that to do with it?"

"I don't want people to say I am allowing my daughter to run after a married man."

"But surely they will if you invite them here. If you leave matters as they are, no one will get the opportunity."

"Do you think Maureen MacLaverty will keep her mouth shut? It will be the talk of the town that Merton Sandys met you and made this play an excuse to see more of you."

"I shall ask him to give up the idea if that is what will happen. You have spoilt everything. Why does everything have to become the subject of wretched gossip?"

Maeve stared at her mother across a barricade of mounting dislike. But Kate noticed nothing. "How does Maud like it? I should have thought she wouldn't want you to trespass on her preserves."

"There is no use in discussing it, Mummy. Merton is a friend of Maud's brother, a friend who has come to take a rest. He is not married, if you must know. I don't think Maud regards him as her private property, and I should hate him to think that a man in Ireland is like a stag at bay."

Kate softened. It was something to be confided in even to this extent. It suggested that by adopting another line she might get a little further into Maeve's confidence.

"You mustn't take me up so literally, Maeve. You can have no idea what it is like to live in this family where no one shares anything. Your father is out all day. John has become a complete stranger, using the house as an hotel: faith, if it were an hotel he would give the management more information than he gives me. I don't know when to expect him. The babies are off with their granny for the holidays. They like it better there. And I can't blame them. But it makes me feel no one needs me now. You never tell me anything. You shut me out of your life. And it isn't right. Father Tom was saying the other night how important it was nowadays for parents to take an interest in their children's doings. There is so much immorality in the world at present. He congratulated me, if you please, on the way I ran my home. Little does he know."

"But you don't believe something wrong is going on between me and Merton Sandys, do you?" Maeve was genuinely astonished.

"I have too much faith in you, and the upbringing you have had. But I think you ought to be careful. A man like that would think nothing of having a fling with a girl like yourself. The fact that he is married wouldn't prevent him. You have been brought up in a good home and you don't know how these people behave."

"He is not married."

"I don't believe it . . ."

"He was. But his wife left him. There is a divorce going through. It was his wife who broke up the marriage."

"If he is free to marry, I bet Miss Maud has her eyes on him. The divorce would not upset her. If you want to keep friendly with Maud, keep out of his way. That's my advice to you."

"I don't think Maud has any feelings about him at all. I'm sure she hasn't, in fact."

"Don't tell me if he started to pay her attention she wouldn't jump at him. She is getting on. Well over thirty, I'd say."

"Twenty-nine."

"Twenty-nine is getting on if a girl wants to get married. The men in her set prefer them younger than that. And don't tell me just because she is a peer's daughter Maud doesn't want a man, and won't object to a younger girl getting in her way. You will have to open your eyes, Maeve. You can't remain a child for ever."

"Maud knows lots of people. I should think she could have married long ago if she had wanted to."

"That's the trouble with her sort. They are picky and choosy when they are young. And in the end, very often, they get left. Maud isn't such a beauty. And don't tell me if a man like this gave her half a chance, she will turn it down now. I am sure he is more fun than the sort of old has-beens you meet at Saggart."

Coarse, vulgar and horrible as her mother's remarks seemed to Maeve, they were not devoid of interest. Thoughts which had come to her, to be suppressed as soon as they were born, were now being forcibly resurrected. Maud's manner had certainly changed. After lavishing affection on her that night Merton arrived, she had abruptly retreated into aloofness. But until now Maeve had not connected this with Merton. She had been embarrassed by Maud's demonstrativeness, and had assumed that Maud had been embarrassed herself. That the change arose from another cause, that Maud was jealous, Maeve could not believe. But there was sufficient similarity between her own shy speculations and her mother's blatant guesses to give her unpleasant misgivings.

"Let me ask Merton about the party idea. Perhaps he won't object to it. I don't think its fair to jump it on him."

Maeve, remembering her plans for the next day, saw the advantage of making peace.

"I will see him tomorrow. Why not leave it until then? I have to go into town now. And if Ellen rings up will you tell her I can't go to Fitzwilliam with her tomorrow, I will be out all day."

"There must be something wrong with the telephone, it has been ringing on and off. But when I pick it up there seems to be no one at the other end."

As if it had been listening to this, the telephone rang again. Maeve picked it up.

"Hello," she said.

There was silence, not the incoherence of an erratic system, perfect silence.

"Hello," she said again. And then: "Hello. Hello. Hello."

She thought she heard someone breathing at the end of the telephone. Kate, leaving the room, said:

"It's been doing that to me. You should report it."

"This is Maeve O'Connell. Who is that?" said Maeve as soon as she was alone.

A voice said, "I want to see you. Could you meet me this evening in Dublin?"

"I am going out this evening. I could meet you this afternoon at any time you like."

"Four o'clock on the bridge in Stephen's Green."

"Very well."

The comfortable feeling engendered by the talk with Merton had been dispelled by the return of Mr Kelly. It was the difference between life and death.

It was five minutes to four when Maeve had completed her arrangements to get her car across the Border in the morning. She entered the park by the Dawson Street gate and had the bridge in view at once. A woman with an overcrowded pram stood musing on the bridge. There was no sign of Mr Kelly. Maeve crossed the bridge and looked along the rows of deck chairs to see if he was there. She waited for half an hour: and then walked diagonally across the Green to the Leeson Street gate where her car was parked. When she came to the fountain over which three Teutonic females, representing the Fates, preside, someone touched her elbow. Maeve started.

"I was going away. I waited half an hour," she said.

Kelly made no reply to this, but continued at her side. He was shorter than she by at least an inch, but was strongly built. He wore a hat of green furry felt which suited his pale face no better than his suit of blue grey cloth. He looked like a country schoolmaster in Dublin for a conference.

"This is my car," said Maeve at last. As Kelly made no comment, she got in. He stood at the window.

"Do you still want to help Sean?" he said.

"I told you so. I meant what I said."

"When can you go?"

"I am driving a friend of mine tomorrow to Enniskillen where he is lunching. After that I am free. But what I cannot understand is why Johnny is held up there. The Border is not closed. Anyone can pass through."

Kelly fixed Maeve with his dyspeptic stare. Then he said:

"Your brother was followed to the place where he is now. The district is cordoned off. They can't find him. But if he moves, they will. They have his fingerprints. Tomorrow is a good day. There is weekend traffic. Sean is at the house of a man called Peter Murphy in Clones. It is beside a public house—O'Neill's. If you call at O'Neill's ask to see Peter. You will recognise him easily by his hare-lip. I will get a message through. Talk to nobody else. If you are caught keep your mouth shut.

Keep your mouth shut anyway. Who is this friend you are driving to Enniskillen?"

"Merton Sandys."

"Who is he?"

"The actor."

"I seem to know the name."

"He is a well-known actor."

"Is he English?"

"Yes."

"How long have you known him?"

"I met him recently."

"He may be one of their spies. Did he suggest this trip?"

"I did. I can assure you Merton is not a spy. He is one of the many people who are not interested in Irish politics. He doesn't know anything about them. He thinks the reason why Ireland is divided is because Carson defeated de Valera in the Civil War."

"I should like to know more about him. We can take no risks."

"Have some common sense. Did you ever hear of an actor who was a secret service agent? I don't mean to be rude but I think Merton would regard any time spent on Irish politics as wasted."

Kelly gave his approximation of a smile.

"I don't know many stage actors," he said.

"I will answer for Merton Sandys."

"The password is B.B.C. Unless you say that Dan won't listen or talk."

Maeve repeated aloud "Peter Murphy's place. O'Neill's pub. B.B.C." Then: "Goodbye," she said.

"Slán leat," said Kelly (which in Irish means goodbye).

At home her father noticed her air of suppressed excitement and wondered to himself. Kate was on the telephone the whole evening discussing plans with her fellow committee women and noticed nothing.

"The play has been mislaid by the publishers. What are we going to do?" she said to Dan after an hour's discussion with Molly Pratt.

"The Mikado. People always enjoy it. They know the tunes," he said.

Kate rolled her eyes and rushed back to the telephone. Her family were no use, no use at all in this crisis. But she loved the excitement, the alarums, the clash of battle: the anti-rheumatism campaign was filling, in her case certainly, a long-felt want.

*   *   *

"Miss Tuffy, that dreadful man has sent a telegram threatening action if we don't find his wretched play. Are you sure you looked through the files?—thoroughly, I mean."

"I stayed in for three hours last night, Sir Walter. I was never given that play."

"But look at the telegram, Miss Tuffy."

"I can't help it, Sir Walter. Are you sure there was a play in the brown paper parcel? People don't wrap up plays in parcels like that."

"He did, Miss Tuffy. We must find it."

"I told you, Sir Walter, I have looked everywhere. I must say . . ."

"Please, Miss Tuffy. There's no need to burst into tears over it. How do you think I feel? This will cost the firm thousands. I always live to regret it when I disobey my instinct. And my instinct was not to give that fellow a penny for the damn thing."

"May I go, Sir Walter?"

"By all means. But do keep an eye out, won't you?"

Miss Tuffy raced from the room.

"I wonder could I tactfully suggest she sees a doctor. I'm sure they have something that helps at these times," he thought.

The telephone rang.

"Will you take a trunk call from Dublin, Sir Walter?"

"From Dublin. No. Yes. Who is it? Mangan. Yes. I said I would take it. Yes. YES. I said YES. Damn this telephone. Oh, Mangan, is that you? Yes. I got your telegram."

CHAPTER XIII

MAEVE DROVE WITH savage intensity along the northern road. She was angry. Merton, pretending not to notice this, lay back and admired the scenery. They had not spoken for ten minutes: when his ejaculations of pleasure at the modest scenery on the route had elicited no response, he gave up making them and lit a pipe. Perhaps he had been patronising, giving the impression that a few fatherly words should have been all that Maeve required to dissuade her from her project. Perhaps he had failed to guess the strength of her feelings.

"If it was your brother," she said, "you would leave him without help while you went off for the weekend to enjoy yourself, would you?"

"If you were my sister I should be furious with you for involving yourself in my affairs. Your brother took this silly business up. He did not consult you. The last thing he would want would be this added responsibility. He took his chance. That, I am sure, is his attitude; as it would be mine."

"If he were drowning, and he were your brother, you would not dive in to try to save him? Would you? The argument is the same."

"One is an accident."

"The danger is the same. And I am fond of my brother. I don't suppose you know what it is to be fond of somebody."

It was when the conversation got to this point, Merton had recourse to his pipe.

An hour later he suggested that he should drive. Maeve who had not slept for two nights showed signs of strain. Twice the car had gone up on the grass margin of the road. At first Maeve refused. Then, feeling she was being, after all, something of a child, she gave him the wheel.

It had been agreed that Maeve should lunch at the Wagstaff's house with Merton. It was wonderful cover for her. Wagstaff was a retired British diplomat who had settled down in Enniskillen with his wife, a rich woman, who encouraged him to entertain and keep in touch with the world. Merton had met them when he was film-making in the Middle East before Sir William's retirement.

"Are you sure they won't feel I am imposing on them?" Maeve inquired. She had been surprised at the assurance with which Merton had proposed bringing her to a party to which she had not been invited.

"They were delighted when I suggested it. This party is a semi-official 'do' apparently. A lot of the Northern top brass. Pretty grim. You will add to the light relief and set off the practical Northern wives. William is a wonderful old boy. He said he was sure you were pretty."

"That is a reflection on you."

"Is it? I like beauty. I like beautiful people."

"I am not beautiful."

"That is true."

"Thank you."

"Not classically beautiful. But wonderfully pretty. I only know two women who are as pretty as you."

"And who are they?" she asked coldly.

"Now that I come to think of it, they are not so pretty. Are you glad?"

"Oh, immensely relieved."

But she had no heart for Merton's flippancy. Her spirits had drooped. In the ordinary course, what could have been pleasanter than the prospect of a day in the country with him? For spoiling that, she held Tony Kelly responsible, a whipping boy for John. She intended after luncheon was over to call on the hare-lipped Peter and improvise. The fact that she had no plan to worry over made it seem easier to put through the social effort ahead of her. She wondered uneasily how John would behave when she found him. In the old days he had fiercely resented what he called 'the big sister act'. Nothing in the past had resembled this. He might refuse to accept her help from pure cussedness.

The Customs formalities at the Border did not take long, nor could Maeve see any indication of police activity. But on the other side she saw cars being held up and the drivers questioned. As her own car had an Eire plate and was a conspicuous shade of duck egg blue, she thought well to stop occasionally and ask the direction to Sir William Wagstaff's house and how long it would take to get there.

"What are you up to?" said Merton when the third lot of Ulster Specials had been interrogated.

But Maeve did not answer him.

It was that rare thing a fine summer day. And in its honour Wagstaff's guests were being served their aperitifs on a lawn at the side of the house. Sir William was proud of his roses and liked them as a setting. He came forward to greet Merton and his companion, blowing with affability. A man in full bloom, whose bright complexion had defied all foreign suns. His wife was decorative in her own way, more austere than her husband, 'a good fellow' first and a man of consequence afterwards. She belonged to that almost vanished race of women who have the appearance of having always commanded a household of servants. It derived in part from three years in India when she first married; but it would have been there had she never left her own country. As Merton had been warned the guests were mostly officials of the Northern Government. But some were neighbours. Merton (and Maeve because she came with him) obviously excited curiosity.

Merton was set far apart from Maeve at the table. She had beside her on the right a worthy man who had expert knowledge of public hygiene, and when not discussing that, compared the relative merits of two north of Ireland hotels as holiday resorts. On her other side was a silent man who ate with a certain intensity, pausing at fixed intervals to run his napkin across his mouth. When he drank he showed the same sense of deliberateness. After each swallow he brought his tumbler down on the table with the smartness of a guardsman presenting arms.

On a few occasions Maeve tried to gather the necessary courage to begin conversation with this neighbour but she could never catch his eye, so she gave it up and resigned herself to the talkative one. An appearance of attention satisfied his purpose: she had long since ceased to listen to him and interested herself in looking round the table. Nowhere could she see anyone who in the least resembled Merton's description of his host for the weekend. Sometimes Merton caught her eye. He was looking enormously serious while a large lady discussed the government's educational programme. As the meal proceeded Maeve found herself looking more and more at Merton. She was sorry she had not managed the morning better. She need not have been so cross. She wondered if he liked her less for it.

To her amazement a firm pressure on her left knee proved, when she inspected the cause, to have been applied by the intense eater. He had finished eating for the moment.

"Terrible weather we have been having lately," he said.

"Yes," said Maeve, "but today is nice."

By suddenly stretching out her leg she freed her knee but in doing so she kicked a sad-looking woman opposite who gave a short scream of pain.

"I am so sorry," said Maeve.

"It's me varicose vein," said the woman, but without excessive rancour.

Finding a vacuum where his hand had been, Maeve's neighbour surfaced again. Soon he was busy with a toothpick. But he was not finished with conversation.

"You are on the stage, too," he said, nodding towards Merton.

"No."

"Just interested on account of your friend?"

"I come from Dublin."

"I was thinking there was a wee touch of the south in your voice. How are you getting on down there?"

"Quite well. Thank you."

"I wish you would keep your I.R.A. men in order. They are a proper headache, I don't mind telling you!"

"Do you live near the Border?"

"I do not. I live in Belfast. And I would have a quiet life if it were not for these fellows. You should keep them in order down there."

"I wish I could."

"What I say is : 'You are as much entitled to your religion as I am to mine'."

"That is very liberal of you."

"It's the way I am made. What I say is : 'We both worship

the same God even though your religion may not be the same as mine'."

"I see what you mean."

"The other fellow may disagree with me, but that doesn't mean I can't like him. We have a saying in Ulster: 'It takes all kinds to make a world'."

"There is a great deal in that."

"It's the way I am made. I take no credit for it. I have met many a decent Catholic man. I have a friend who is a Catholic. I always say to him, 'John, you have your ideas. I have mine. But that doesn't prevent me from thinking you are a decent man'."

The waiter, bearing claret, relieved Maeve from the necessity of replying. When he had replenished their glasses, she noticed that her neighbour's eyes were slightly suffused at the picture of his own disposition.

"What I say is: 'It doesn't matter in the long run what a man is if he is a decent man. Ask anyone about me and I think you will find they will say: 'You can trust Andy Clune. He is a decent man.' Do you like this claret?"

"It's good. What is it? I don't know much about wine."

"This is the seventeen and sixpenny."

"Fancy."

"Are you staying up north for long?"

"I go back after lunch."

"You should stay longer than that. I would ask you to come and see my place, but I have to drive to Newry this afternoon. Your boys have been giving us trouble there."

"I hope they haven't damaged any property of yours."

"Not of mine exactly. But I'm in charge of the police in those parts."

"I didn't know. I know very little about the north, I'm afraid."

"You should come oftener. We would give you a good time. A pretty face is the only passport a nice wee girl requires."

As though stamping the document, he laid his hand on Maeve's knee.

"A policeman's life is not a happy one," he said.

This time she took his hand and gently, but firmly, removed it.

"I don't know exactly what you mean by a passport."

"Perhaps I mean a recommendation. You must not think of us up here as dull folk. There's better crack in the north than you'll find anywhere. We have a saying in the north 'All work and no play makes Jack a dull boy'."

"I have often heard you quoted."

"I daresay."

"I don't suppose you would like to come to Newry," said the police chief who had been working on his teeth again.

"I am meeting my brother," said Maeve. "I am not sure what his plans are."

"Is he working up in these parts?"

"Yes. For the B.B.C."

"Ah! They are a queer lot."

"My brother is not officially B.B.C. It's a free-lance assignment."

"I'd like to know what he's doing. I don't trust that crowd. They seem to be recruited from Sinn Feiners, judging by the things they let people say about us. I hope he isn't going to misrepresent us. I'd like to talk to him."

Later Merton said: "Mossy never made it. You will have to come with me now. God moves in a mysterious way."

Later, Maeve said: "You can take my car. Here is the key. Reverse is up and to the left. I am going to Newry with a member of the R.U.C. He wants to discuss the B.B.C. with my brother. God moves in a mysterious way."

Later. Maeve getting out of a motor-car, the property of the Royal Ulster Constabulary, said: "I promised to meet my brother in here. Don't you move. I will fetch him. I hope you don't mind taking part in a pub crawl at this time of day."

Later. The police chief said: "I did not want to say anything at the time, but that is not the sort of place you ought to go into. That pub has a bad name. My men are watching it. It's a Sinn Fein house. That is what I mean about the B.B.C. They go to a Sinn Fein pub, collect a story from some I.R.A.

sympathiser, and then broadcast it to the world. I am very glad I have had the opportunity to warn you."

Later. As the train left Newry station John said, "What do you think you are doing, Maeve? I wish you would mind your own business."

Later, Maeve said: "We have crossed the Border now. I feel very sleepy. I think I shall fall asleep."

CHAPTER XIV

"THIS IS MONSTROUS. Miss Tuffy. Miss Tuffy."

"Yes, Sir Walter."

"A letter from some Dublin solicitor about this accursed manuscript."

"Have you looked at home, Sir Walter?"

"Really, Miss Tuffy."

"I can think of no other solution unless he took it away himself."

"We have been over all that a dozen times. I should never have seen him. I knew it. Sitting there menacing me until I paid him. Yes, I actually paid him to go away. And now this. You had better put everything else aside until you find it."

"I have told you a thousand times, Sir Walter. I have not got that manuscript. Despite this I have searched everywhere it could have been if I had had it. I can do no more. I have been late now for three evenings."

"You must not take it so personally, Miss Tuffy. I have trouble enough, God knows."

"I am afraid I must give notice, Sir Walter. I can't endure another week like the last. I must consider my health. I am sorry after so many years."

"But this is absurd."

"I have made up my mind. I am sorry."

"It is so unreasonable. You don't have any responsibility in the matter."

"I am sorry. It is not for me to suggest a successor: but if it's any help I think I should tell you that some of the staff in Dangerfields are leaving on account of the policy of that firm. They don't like being associated with the type of book Dangerfields is publishing. It is only a suggestion. I won't bother you about a reference at the moment. But you will let me have one I hope."

Miss Tuffy raced from the room. Sir Walter buried his face in his hands.

* * *

"Why aren't you ready? What has you wandering round in your skin with half Dublin on the door-step? I don't know what's come over you lately; you don't seem to be in it at all."

Kate had come upstairs to find Maeve standing disconsolate in her dressing-gown. The cocktail party, allegedly to forward the interests of the anti-rheumatism campaign, but actually to show Merton off, was due to begin in a quarter of an hour.

"Someone must have been helping themselves to my things. I can't find a pair. These are past praying for."

"I'd have thought you were old enough by now to buy your own clothes. Anyway I haven't time to go rummaging through linen now. I don't suppose you'll catch your death of cold if you go without them. There's a drawer full of my things here if you can find anything to fit you."

Kate's rather blowsy personality was contradicted by extreme neatness in her personal habits. Maeve who had a fastidious nature was slap-dash and untidy. The contrast between her room which looked as if a bomb had recently exploded there—books, papers and clothes scattered over the floor and tables—and Kate's, where everything was arranged and ordered, was surprising.

Maeve dived into a drawer and pulled out layers of silk carefully wrapped in tissue paper smelling hygienically of anti-moth precautions. Kate had never thrown away or given away a garment.

"These will do if I had a pin. They'll fall down as they are."

"Here, take this, alannah," said Kate taking a nappy-pin from another repository. "Hurry up for God's sake. I don't want to be left to cope on my own with all your grand friends."

A few seconds later Maeve was startled by a shriek from her mother's room. Standing at the window she had observed a compact group of poor relations turning in the gate, determined not to miss a moment of the entertainment. They would be the last to go, complicating the supper arrangements that were playing round in Kate's mind. She hoped that Dan wouldn't jib at the idea of taking a select party to the Russell when the cocktails were disposed of.

"Will you look at her for God's sake. She must be ninety if she's a day."

Kate was addressing the air, as Maeve had gone back to her room.

Very slowly, but with the pertinacity of a hedgehog crossing a lawn, Lady Kilmacud was toiling up the steps. The grin that she put on with her gold wig for parties was firmly fixed on her face. A rose spot on each cheek lit up the prevailing yellow. The poor relations watched her progress with ill-concealed curiosity and wonder.

Kate gave a quick final look at herself in the glass. As usual, her own appearance put her in good conceit with herself. If she showed signs of age, her vitality was there. In her coarsened features and thickened figure it was more in evidence than when she was less emphatically formed and moulded.

* * *

The roar in the room had grown so intense no one could hear what anyone else was saying. Even to lift a glass was dangerous: invariably an elbow sent the contents over the front of a dress or down a waistcoat. Smoke lay on the air, giving the final touch of a battlefield to the scene. Red-eyed, hoarse and martini-stained, Maeve sought refuge for a moment in the school-room. At the bottom of the stairs, beside the kitchen, it opened out on the garden, and, in comparison with the turmoil in the rooms upstairs, it breathed an air of restfulness and peace. She was surprised to find Maud and John sitting on cushions in the french window.

"We have been having a lovely time, darling," said Maud. "I was prowling and I found this heavenly room. Johnny was very selfishly keeping it to himself. Is Merton still alive? I saw a very menacing couple driving him into a corner, and I must say I despaired for him. I suppose he regards it all as part of the rest cure. Is there any hope of rescuing him and bringing him down here? Just the four of us. It would be so nice to be talking quietly listening to the room above our heads. It reminds me of our air-raid shelter in London during the blitz.

Who is the poppet with the beard? He was trying to get a nice fat priest through the crowd to introduce him to that nymphet in the corner. I don't think the priest was built for a party this size. He got horribly wedged in the process, fossilised by now I should think. Poor dear."

Maeve looked at her brother to see how he was reacting to Maud's party manner. She expected an explosion, but to her surprise, John seemed, for once, to be content. He looked neither injured nor derisive. But he did look as he used to when Maeve tried to join in his games with friends whom he brought home from school. Girls were out of place on those occasions. And Maeve quite obviously was out of place now, so she drank in some air at the open window and went back to her mother's party. At this distance it sounded like a crowd scene in a film of the French Revolution, the prelude to an attack on the Bastille. But when she opened the drawing-room door the sound rushed out like a tidal wave overwhelming and drowning her. And when she shut herself in with the red-faced, sweating, screaming mob, she felt suddenly desperately lonely.

It was no use trying to get near Merton. Her mother's face, looked triumphant, bobbed up and down in the crowd. The fat priest was standing in front of a pretty old lady saying something which she could not hear, each sentence punctuated by a buffet from his stomach as the crowd swayed into the seat of his black cloth trousers. At each push from his stomach the old lady was hurled backwards against Mangan the poet who acted as a buffer, giving a little with each impact, so that his face drew nearer to Molly's and then receded in a rhythm which—she had taken quite a lot—had a disturbingly aphrodisiacal effect on her. She, too, could not hear what he was saying. But it was better so; for his complaints about the absence of whiskey were not in keeping with her ecstatic mood.

By half past eight it was all over. The peace of the desert had descended upon the house. Dan moodily shifted his glance from the empty bottles and glasses to the carpet stains and cigarette burns. Merton, looking wan, sought Maeve's eyes imploringly. John, fascinated, was staring at Maud who alone looked fresh and cool, contrasting as strongly with the women who had borne the burden and heat of the day as would a flower brought in from the garden with the wilting decorations of the smoke-laden, gin-breathing, battered rooms. Lady Kilmacud, Maureen MacLaverty, Molly Pratt and Francis Xavier Mangan stood in a decorative group against the fireplace which now had the appearance of a mammoth ashtray. Kate, tired but triumphant, advanced on her husband. "Bring out the champagne, Dan," she whispered. He hesitated, as a donkey will resist the first urgings of its rider. "Quickly," she hissed. "Or everybody will go."

It did not seem a well-considered reason for acting. But it was sufficient.

"No sign of the play yet?" Merton inquired.

"That publisher should be shot," said Molly.

"I have put my solicitor on to him. That ought to do the trick. You can't trust any of these fellows. You wouldn't know what they are up to," Mangan felt in a self-assertive mood. With each day his confidence increased. If the manuscript had really disappeared Sir Walter would pay through the nose rather than have the publicity of an action. The possibility made Mangan glow with an almost patriotic fervour. It was as if he were being given the opportunity to avenge in person every national grievance from the Famine to the Casement diaries. Sir Walter would have to bear the burden of his nation's guilt. Mangan had never liked the man before. Now the thought of him lifted his heart. But there were dreadful, deflated moments when the possibility that the manuscript might be found loomed up. But this evening Mangan drowned the thought in champagne and concentrated on changing the subject whenever Merton, who took his profession seriously, questioned him on the theme of the play. Mangan was vague. The idea of the play was really symbolical. A description in a few words was only misleading. There were many themes, inter-locking as it were. He gesticulated impatiently in the manner of one who is being talked to and is at the same time trying to carry on a telephone conversation.

"Is there a principal character?"

"That's what the actor always wants to know." Mangan gave a tired smile at Dan, who started anxiously. He had lost touch with the conversation.

"What's that?" he said.

"You can't really blame an actor for wanting to know, can you?" said Merton suavely.

"That's right," said Dan weightily, to emphasise that the last remark had had his full attention.

Mangan shrugged and made another movement with his hand as though he were throwing grain to importunate chickens. "You can't *blame* them. But you can say that this subordination of the play to the actor is the mark of the commercial theatre. It strikes at the heart of the movement which Yeats and Lady Gregory founded. All I am trying in my small way to do is to keep faith with that tradition."

"But couldn't you tell us what the play is about?" said Dan ingenuously.

Mangan sighed. "I tell you you would be no better off. You are not children who want a story. Mr Sandys is not an unemployed man begging for a job at the Labour Exchange. I am not a smart alec trying to get a synthetic concoction on in the London West End. If we were those things I would say: it's the story of Ireland's defeat: the great tradition is personified by Carolan the blind harper who is there throughout the play as himself and at times as others—as Owen Roe, as Sarsfield, as Tone, as Mitchel, as Parnell and as Yeats."

"Yeats?" cried Maureen MacLaverty. "I thought you were going to say de Valera."

Mangan smiled grimly. "You will not be the only one."

"And is the one actor to play all the parts?" asked Mrs MacLaverty who gave the impression of not perfectly understanding.

"Yes and no. That is why you can't discuss the play like this."

"But surely when the parts are being given out each will know what he is playing," said Kate who was naturally suspicious of vagueness.

A wave of anger passed over the poet's face. "If you like, one actor plays Carolan the blind harper."

"Christopher Casson," said Kate and smiled for Molly's approval. But Molly had her eyes on Mangan. She knew he was on the edge of an outburst.

"And then others will play Tone, Parnell, etc.," said Kate to Lady Kilmacud who was nodding happily, listening to nothing, and delighted with everything.

"If you will forgive me, they will do nothing of the kind," said Mangan sharply.

"Oh, I beg your pardon."

"That is my whole point. Their characters will merge in Carolan's who alone will carry through the generations the spirit of the tradition. They will be themselves and they will be him."

"Faith, Father Tom will be required to explain that to us," said Dan cheerfully. "It will need more than a bit of shamrock."

"Here, fill up. You'll need it after that."

He poured some champagne into Mangan's glass. The poet allowed this, but he lay back in his chair in a frightful sulk.

"We must read it. Then it will be clear," said Kate.

Mangan snorted.

"Time is the problem," said Merton. "I was talking to Milton last night; and we both agree that unless we start rehearsing by the middle of August we won't be able to put a show on in September. And I am off to Portugal to make a film at the end of September. Have you not got the original manuscript, Mr Mangan? We could get it typed again."

Mangan nodded. "I don't know where it is."

"It ought to be in the National Library," said Molly.

Everyone present signified their assent to this by little murmurs of approval.

"I wish Milton were here," said Kate who had become on Christian name terms with all the theatrical personalities of Dublin in the course of a week.

"I expected to see him," said Maureen MacLaverty.

"He is rehearsing a play for a convent in Blackrock," said Kate. "I don't know how he fits it all in."

"He thinks we ought to have an alternative ready if Mr Mangan's play is not recovered by the end of the week," said Merton.

"Just a precaution," said Kate who had noticed Mangan's rising anger.

"Musicals do best in Dublin," said Dan who had his own opinions on the theatre.

"Dan, dear. It's getting very late. Would you ring up the Russell and book a table for us," said Kate. She hoped to forestall the suggestion of *The Mikado* which she felt was imminent.

Dan without marked enthusiasm rose to do his wife's bidding. "For how many?" he asked ruefully.

Kate counted. "Eight. Oh, I was forgetting John and Maud. That will be ten. Say we will be there at 9.30."

Dan made his way to the telephone. Dinner for ten at the Russell. Added to the champagne which was being lowered at surprising speed considering all that had gone before, he would have spent enough already to stamp out rheumatism for ever. And this was only the beginning. His eye happened to catch the expensive picture upon which the setting sun momentarily gleamed; a sudden revulsion against his mode of life swept over Dan. Buying things he did not want; entertaining people he did not care for; planning the production of a play which was certain to bore him. Why did he let himself be swept along by this stream? Where was it going? He very nearly put his red fist through the picture which symbolised for him the insincerity of his life. But, as always, restrained himself in time. He would do his wife's bidding, his wife who had caught him once in the springe of the flesh and laid him under tribute for ever.

The telephone at the Russell was engaged. It took him ten minutes to make his call. When he returned the women were eagerly discussing a new play which an actress friend of Merton's had written.

"She might jump at the chance to try it out," he was saying when Dan returned. "And might even act in it. I don't think it will amount to much, but she is a bright girl and it will be fairly amusing from what I hear."

"Hazel Twigg may be coming, Dan. We will have the Edinburgh Festival in the tuppenny place soon," cried Kate excitedly.

"Can't the woman shut up," thought Molly, looking at Mangan.

"Damn them all. Damn them all. I hope that bloody fellow finds the play now," thought Mangan, glaring back at her.

"If we are to get anything to eat we had better be on the move," said Dan.

"Yahs. Yahs," said Lady Kilmacud, who, ever since the Russell had been mentioned, had been flapping like a dusty hen.

It was the first time she had spoken.

"Whatever happens, we must see that Maurice O'Leary keeps his promise to recite *Tara* in Irish," said Maureen MacLaverty in a confidential tone to Mangan as they made their way out. She was notorious in her circle for her tact.

* * *

"The old cow," said Mangan as he rolled into Molly's little Morris. He was referring to Mrs MacLaverty but would have transferred the epithet to any of her friends.

"I want to go round by the flat," said Molly.

When she got there, she stopped the car but did not get out immediately. She had not enjoyed the conversation at Kate's and she dreaded the epilogue in the Russell. The enthusiasm with which the idea of a play by this actress, Hazel Twigg, had been greeted, had not escaped her, nor its effect on Mangan's saturnine disposition. He might become so aggressive this evening that the committee would throw him over. They were longing to. She knew that. She thought it was very unkind of Merton Sandys to bring up the idea of a desirable alternative until the last possible moment.

"Do you want to eat at the Russell?" she said.

"The food is good, I hear. I can't afford the place myself."

"But are you in the mood for more talk? Those women . . . the noise. I could slap up one of your omelettes. And I have a bottle of our Remy Martin."

If Mangan could have eaten alone in the Russell, or with that pretty O'Connell girl, he had no doubt what he would choose to do. But the prospect of *those women,* that smooth actor with his know-all air, Dan O'Connell's solecisms, that self-confident Mountstephen bitch, Molly's anxious stare—all this was a heavy price to pay for even the best French cooking. And he was tired.

But there were advantages in a public hotel, he would be in a crowd, and yet alone in a way that he could not be with Molly. But it is easier to fall than to fight. And he was tired.

"I think it would be nicer here," he said after an unflattering pause.

"Good. So do I. They won't miss us in the crowd. Come along."

Once in the flat their behaviour followed a pattern, an established routine. Mangan lounged in the best chair, his feet up and a drink in his hand while Molly set to work in the kitchen, singing snatches, popping in and out to see how her man was, calling out to him that all went well, busy and happy cosseting him. Mangan could relax. Inevitably a moment came when the brandy was finished, general topics exhausted and the light had gone. Left to itself the evening would have died. And he was tired.

The brandy and the intimacy of the room and Molly insinuating tenderness overcame his resistance. He seemed to lose his identity, to wander in a faint haze. The outlines of Molly's face, of the furniture of the room itself became blurred. He was grateful when Molly helped him on to the bed, loosened his tie, unlaced his shoes, and eased him gently and expertly out of his clothes as if she were peeling a chestnut; then, with a quick rough movement she unfastened something on herself, slipped off her dress and lay beside him, stroking the back of his grizzled head, murmuring in his ear.

Nothing mattered now; over his head the waters closed shutting out the hostile faces. All was peace now. In his ears the soft sound of receding waters melted gradually away.

"Frank!"

A gentle sussuration, as from an infant asleep at the breast, answered her, to be followed by another and another, each louder than the one before, until the tight-shuttered, cluttered room seemed too small to contain such a volume of sound, such a compression of air.

*   *   *

Maeve hoped to drive Merton to the Russell but hadn't reckoned with Maud. It was odd when the girls were such friends that Maud never helped in any of these manoeuvres. Rather the contrary; and for some reason, based on instinct, Maeve was shy to ask for her assistance.

John's surprising and unconcealed fascination with Maude made him a more promising ally.

"You go with her," Maeve said, "and let me drive Merton in yours." It was the measure of John's passion that he was ready immediately to hand over his new car to his sister. Maud was less co-operative.

"I don't see why we need take two cars. You can all fit in with me," she said.

"I want to try out Johnny's car. I won't get another chance."

"Be careful of her. Or I'll never forgive you," John said, getting in beside Maud.

"Will you get in behind, Merton," Maud said with that glacial air which Maeve had begun to dread.

But Merton pretended not to hear, and followed Maeve back to the garage.

"Oh damn! How silly of me. I never asked him for the key."

She ran out on the road, but the last of the cars had driven away.

"We can ring up a taxi."

The house was empty, all around the desolation that follows in the wake of a party. Glasses half empty, in some of which cigarette ends obscenely floated. Plates of half consumed pâtés and cheese straws, lonely olives. Everywhere cluttered with forlorn remnants. Stains on the camel-coloured carpet.

"He might have left the key in his room. He had on a sports coat when he came in," Maeve said. "I'll go up and look."

"You stay here," she added when Merton moved to accompany her. "He won't want you to see what a mess his room is in," she added. Until then she had been behaving unselfconsciously; but this made her suddenly aware that she was alone in the house with him. The hired help had gone. Down in the kitchen Mrs Murphy was solacing her niece, who had come in to help, with a cup of tea and miscellaneous snacks collected like tithes from the plates on their way upstairs from the kitchen.

Maeve searched in her brother's pockets and poked round among the objects scattered over his room. He was as untidy in his way as she was in hers. She did not like to rummage in case she might come across secrets. But she purposely delayed because she wanted to get rid of the feeling that she had had ever since Merton offered to help in the search. A pleasurable terror.

There was no sign of the key.

Downstairs Merton was thoughtfully clearing away the debris. This was one of the things about him that Maeve particularly liked. It was simple and kind, showing how unspoilt he was by success. It also made her feel less in awe of him.

"It's not there," Maeve said. "He must have taken it with him. I daren't ring up and ask him to come back with it. We'll have to get a taxi."

"Is there any need to hurry? I'm rather dreading an evening with old Maud. She was looking pretty sour."

"Perhaps Johnny will put her in good humour. I hope he doesn't get too daft about her. It's quite absurd. She's old enough to be his mother."

"I don't remember Maud when she was nine. But I am sure even then she was too precocious to became a mother."

"I don't think you like her. You are always hinting things. She's my best friend. Why are you staring at me like that?"

"I can never quite make up my mind how innocent you are."

"I don't know what you mean."

Maeve blushed. She was put out.

"Nobody's innocent nowadays," she said.

Merton looked at her again quickly, as if making a decision.

"Johnny may rape her. His I.R.A. training can be put to a benevolent purpose for once. It might do Maud good. Life at Saggart with that dotty miser of a father and her *hausfrau* mother must be hell."

Maeve smiled and tried to look sophisticated. To employ her nervous fingers she began to eat olives.

"Let's dine off the remains. Nobody will miss us at the hotel," Merton said.

Maeve could not see their absence being treated with such amiable indifference. She knew all too well that her mother was longing to be seen with the famous actor in an expensive restaurant. There would be questions asked, and recriminations. Her father would not be harsh, but that injured hound look which she knew so well would follow her round for days. As for Maud . . .

But she was on the edge of the board now and she was not going to step back.

"I'm sure there's something in the fridge," she said. "You can rummage in the sideboard and see if Daddy has left us anything fit to drink."

She found some ham and a huge consignment of sausages in

reserve for the party and not called upon. There was lettuce and some fruit, a hunk of cake and a packet of 'rich digestive biscuits'.

She put a match to the fire, and they ate picnic fashion in front of it. Merton had discovered a bottle of champagne.

"We might as well be hanged for a sheep as a lamb," Maeve said.

"The fire is nearly out. I'm too comfortable to stir," Maeve said.

Merton was stroking her neck. She lay in his arms, happy, not thinking. The world had stopped. She hoped it would never begin again. This was heaven.

Merton's mind was working quite actively, and the dreamy expression in his eyes misled Maeve when she thought that it matched her own. He was not quite sure what his feelings were for Maeve. She was wonderfully fresh and attractive, like a day in the country. He was certainly half in love with her; but there was a factor which he did not usually have to cope with in his affairs that prevented him from letting go. He strongly suspected that she was a virgin. Had he met her in London the idea would not have occurred to him and they would have been in bed long ago. He had not given so much time to any girl for many years without coming to that point. This was part of her fascination. It gave her a nostalgic quality, bringing back the recollections of his Betjemanesque youth, eons and eons ago.

And he was forty, twice her age probably. The deflowering of virgins wasn't in his line. He had an aversion to the idea. Moreover he knew very well that she was in love with him. This increased his sense of responsibility and irked his conscience. He was kind and easy-going, and selfish without any liking for causing pain. Infinite tolerance all round was his ideal for life.

If he let go, it would bring up the dreadful apparition of marriage. And he had had enough of that. Instinct told him that he could get his way with her, but it also warned that she would equate that with love and love with marriage. He had divined an immense innocence. Quite clearly she had failed to diagnose Maud's trouble. It all fitted in with what he had heard about Ireland, its celibacy and censorship; but her innocence also prevented her from realising that she was working him up. It was she who should put the shutters up if she didn't want it, it was unreasonable to expect him to refuse to push an open door. He had better make sure. Whatever happened he mustn't lose control of the situation.

In Maeve's conscience a struggle was going forward. If she did not tear herself away now, she wouldn't be able to. She was magnetised, bewitched. The touch of his hand made her shiver, left her powerless. He had slipped her dress over her shoulder and his hands were begining to stray. She made a protesting gesture but cancelled it out by kissing him with a violence which astonished him.

"Darling."

It was the moment of which the priest had spoken, the moment of decision which settles whether you remain on the plain or slide down the hill. The last chance. All you had been taught on one side, the abyss on the other. But the power to decide had left her. *And then she remembered.* She sat up so suddenly that her shoulder hit Merton on the chin with the force of a boxer's knock-out blow.

"I'm sorry. Oh, darling, I'm sorry," she wailed.

He held his head in his hands.

"Did I hurt you? I'm so clumsy. I didn't mean to."

He rocked to and fro. Then he got up, looking pale, and took a trial step.

"I'll be all right in a moment."

"Don't be angry."

"I can't make you out. I don't understand Irish girls. You certainly gave me the wrong impression."

"Go upstairs and take them off," the serpent whispered into Maeve's ear.

But now the magic thread had been broken. And whatever she might have done in hot blood, she couldn't overcome what Kate would have seen as the prevision of St Joseph.

"I didn't think you were a tease."

She wanted to cry.

"Perhaps it's the national passion for guerilla warfare. The surprise attack."

"Don't be beastly."

"I don't think I'm the culprit. Or am I? I'm out of my depth."

He got up then and made it clear that so far as he was concerned the evening was over.

She felt as she had once when she had run over a kitten when she was learning to drive.

"I'll call a taxi for you," she said, surprised at the sound of her own voice. He said nothing.

And she could only stand, desolate, in the hall and watch him open the door and go out when the taxi came.

* * *

Maud made no attempt to talk to John. She had been perfectly friendly—awfully easy to get on with, he thought her—during the party, and made no effort to leave him.

She had a funny way of asking him quite intimate questions. English, he supposed. It emboldened him and helped him to get over his almost paralysing shyness.

He couldn't make out what had annoyed her, unless it was that she was jealous of Merton. She did seem set on having him and Maeve in the car. John had found it distinctly discouraging. He had been quite satisfied with his progress until then. When they arrived at the Russell, Maud stopped the car.

"I can't see anywhere to park," she said.

"The cars thin out if we go back."

They were the first words they had exchanged since they left Tara.

Dan had found a place. Unaware of the scrutiny from Maud's mini, he was following Kate and Lady Kilmacud into the hotel. Suiting their pace to the old lady's, the operation was going to take some time.

"Do you think anyone would miss us if we opted out from the party?" Maud said.

John's heart leaped. Then he remembered that he had come out without any money, and it sunk again. But he wasn't going to fly in the face of Providence.

"I find a little of Lady Kilmacud goes a long way. And I'm cross with Merton," Maud said.

"Why?"

"I think he's being unfair to Maeve."

"She's crazy about him."

"That's what I mean."

"You can't help your feelings, you know."

He hoped that she caught the undertone of his deeply felt remark.

"At the moment I feel that I'm not strong enough to face that gathering. I hope your parents won't be offended. Tell them I had a headache after the cocktail party. Make my peace with them, won't you."

She spoke as if she expected him to leave her.

"I will take you somewhere else," he said. "Where shall we go?"

"You are the man. You make the decisions."

"I must go home first. I'm afraid I left my money behind me."

"Let me take you out."

He shook his head angrily.

"Pride. Pride. I'm older than you, you know."

John hated to hear her say this.

"Let me lend you some money then." She looked in her bag and pulled out two notes. They were not going to go very far on that; but she answered the unspoken query. "Where are the singing pubs, I read so much about? Do take me there. It would be so much nicer than dinner with Senator MacLaverty, don't you think?"

This solved the shortage of funds question. It was bad enough to take a loan, but it would be very embarrassing to have to ask for another.

He suggested a pub in a street quite near the hotel. But as soon as they arrived he realised that it was a mistake.

Maud looked so English and so 'interested', exactly like the Queen, he thought, watching native dances put on for her benefit during tours of her dominions. And then the singing wasn't really very good, nor was the pub in the least attractive. Worst of all, some students with their girls recognised him and their stares made him feel very uncomfortable.

"Do bring them over. I'd love to meet your friends. Are they *all* in the I.R.A.? What nice eyes that dark girl has. I don't think the little plump one should wear *such* tight jeans, do you? It detracts from her nose which is so much the best shaped thing about her."

Reluctant and sulky, John went to fetch his friends. They came up looking unfriendly from shyness; and Maud's efforts to put them at their ease only made them feel small. She certainly belonged to a quite different world. A feeling of dejection and hopelessness swept over him. He sat with his face down, staring at his beer. But Maud looked round her brightly, clapped the singing, and gave John's friends brilliant smiles whenever she caught their eye.

It was not often, because they kept to themselves in a corner and appeared to be talking in whispers. After two hours of what to John had been hell, Maud suddenly seemed to get bored. She asked him quite crossly if he thought Maeve would be at home by now. And they drove back in the same mood as they had set out. He was worrying whether he should hand over the change to Maud or would it be better to wait and send her back two pounds. He was debating this when the car turned in the gate and Maud said suddenly "Buggeration". Just in front of them the O'Connells' Mercedes had drawn up at the steps and Dan was handing out Lady Kilmacud.

* * *

"What time is it?" said Kate.

"Ten fifteen."

"What has happened to everybody?"

"Did you tell them we were coming to the Russell?"

"We mentioned it several times."

"But did we *tell* them? There was so much talk going on this evening, God knows what anybody said or listened to."

"They'd have asked, if they hadn't known. They have tongues in their heads. I hope Maureen MacLaverty is not offended, running off like that as soon as we got here."

"She said she was not feeling well, didn't she?"

"Yes. But—"

"I don't see any reason to *but* about it. The woman is old enough to look after herself."

"Mr Mangan bit the nose off her when she mentioned his poem."

"It's time somebody did. We might as well order something. Soon the restaurant will be empty."

"I think it is an awful anti-climax to be here by ourselves, to invite everyone and to find ourselves with nobody."

"Kate thinks we might as well carry on. If the others turn

up they can join us," said Dan to Lady Kilmacud who sat in the middle of a long table at either end of which the O'Connells presided.

"Exactly," said the old lady. She had been apparently oblivious of her hosts' conversation (as they had of her presence) and contented to sit as long as she was left there, her head turning from side to side, like a ventriloquist's doll; a grin painted on her old face, which tonight looked as if it might crumble away in powder.

Dan called over the waiter and scowled at the menu.

"They have an omelette," he said to Kate as though he had made a useful discovery.

"Oh, very well," she said.

"Vegetables?"

"Spinach and mashed potatoes."

"Very good, sir. For three, sir?"

"You like omelette, Lady Kilmacud?"

"Yahs. Yahs."

"Yes, for three. We will just have coffee afterwards."

"Yes, sir."

The wine-waiter now approached and handed Dan his volume.

Dan looked backwards and forwards through this like one searching for a train in a Bradshaw. Finally, he handed it back.

"That will be all right," he said.

"You will not order anything to drink, sir?"

"No," said Dan.

A look of sulky defiance settled on his face and he cast an aggressive eye around him, not sparing Lady Kilmacud, whose head continued to wag from side to side. Kate held back her tears. It was better, she knew, to concede the battles of no importance in marriage's long war of attrition. But after all the effort she had made, she hardly deserved to be brought down to earth like this. And to find Dan so fundamentally out of sympathy at a moment when she needed his support. He was thinking only of expense, brooding on waste. Admittedly she had done it well. But everything costs money. And Dan had money to spend. Not for the first time there crept into her mind a regretful realisation that she had married a man who was not quite in her own class of life.

CHAPTER XV

"SOME FIRM OF solicitors on the telephone, Sir Walter. They want to know if you would care to nominate another firm to accept service of the writ in the Mangan case."

"They what?"

"Otherwise, they say, they will serve it here."

"A writ for what, may I ask?"

"Damages for the lost manuscript."

"This is outrageous. In all my experience I never met anything like it. My father disliked the Irish. He said they were avaricious and ungrateful. What possessed me to give that ruffian an advance?"

"They are holding on, Sir Walter."

"Tell them to send it to our men. Why do you look so pained, Miss Tuffy? I have to bear the whole brunt of this."

"I have a headache, Sir Walter."

"I beg your pardon. Come back when you have got rid of those people."

"You wanted something, Sir Walter." Miss Tuffy looking strained came back a few minutes later.

"Oh, Miss Tuffy, I hope you have reconsidered your decision. I am afraid this lost manuscript has got in on me too much. I am sorry if I have been unreasonable. What about a change? You look as though you needed a good holiday."

"I have a headache, that is all."

"Have you taken anything for it?"

"I shall take some aspirin when I get home."

"Take it now, Miss Tuffy. Don't wait until you get home."

"I meant to get some at the chemist at lunch-time, but I forgot."

"I used to have some. Let me see. They are probably in this drawer. Pushed at the back most likely. Hello. What's this? By

God. It's Mangan's manuscript. Well, am I not an idiot? It was here under my nose. Did you look in this drawer, Miss Tuffy?"

"I never go to your private drawer, Sir Walter."

"It doesn't matter. Ring up those solicitors and tell them we have it. Say I will send it to Mangan this evening."

"Would it not be as well to ask back the advance first?"

"It's a wonderful idea. But would it be legal?"

"He can't expect you to handle the manuscript after this."

"A rotter like that would expect anything. But I see your point. Tell them we are writing to them. Now what shall I say? Take this down:

Dear Sirs,

We have not had time to obtain our reader's report on Mr Mangan's play—*The Lost Heritage*: but, in any event, we consider that your client's course of action must be interpreted as a severance of relations with our firm. In the absence of a contract, therefore, we must ask for a refund of the advance of £100, made at your client's urgent request. On receipt of this amount, we will post the manuscript to you or to your client as you direct us.

"There. That will make them sit up. Do it right away for me, Miss Tuffy."

"Yes, Sir Walter."

The publisher desired to share his pleasure so he rang up a young actress and asked her to dine with him. She was not acting, had no other engagement, and dearly wanted to publish a mildly erotic novel about life in the Caribbean where she had made a film with Merton Sandys.

That is how Hazel Twigg came to be dining that evening with Sir Walter. No one who saw them together guessed the reason. Miss Twigg allowed Sir Walter to sing his own praises until ten o'clock. Then she introduced the subject of the novel. His brow puckered, but she persevered. He asked her its length and told her that he was not taking on any more fiction. But, when they parted, he told her to send the manuscript and address it to him personally. She declined an invitation to lengthen the evening on the grounds of headache.

On the way home in his taxi, Sir Walter, thinking over the

day, pondered this excuse, it reminded him of Miss Tuffy's headache, until now happily forgotten. I will give her tickets for *My Fair Lady*, he decided. I don't want to lose her to that bounder Dangerfield.

* * *

"I haven't got it, Frank. I am sorry," Mrs Mangan, poised for flight, stopped in the hall to open an American air mail letter.

"The thief won't part with the manuscript unless I pay him. Time is running short."

"Where is the money he gave you?" She seemed to dive from the question into the letter which she had opened without much show of interest.

She had suddenly turned pale.

"Willy's dead."

"Willy?" Mangan always found it difficult to change from the subject which interested him at the moment.

"It's from Mary. Willy died suddenly on her. Heart. He looked an awful colour to me last time they came over. Poor Mary. What will she do? God help her."

"I'm sorry," said Mangan dutifully.

But his wife was concentrating on the letter and his voice trailed off.

"He has left her comfortable. Thank God for that. And listen to this: 'I have the business here. It seems a pity to let it go after the years we spent in building it up. Why wouldn't Frank and yourself come out and share it with me? He could look after the book end, and it would be good for sales to have an author in the shop. I guess he could do with the income. We can manage the business end. Frank, if I know him, won't want to be troubled with that.'"

She put down the letter. "Frank, my prayers must have been listened to. Here is a chance for you. You can make a fresh start in Boston. You will live with books. And we can both make a living. I'm tired of traipsing about, running in and out of the office. I only get a pittance. With my capital I can buy a share in the business. Then you need not feel under a compliment to Mary."

Mangan hesitated. But his hesitation was not indicative of doubt. No one was ever more certain than he that he would prefer death to work in his sister-in-law's book and stationery store. He was hesitating about the form of words only.

"I wonder is Mary wise—to keep on the business, I mean. I've heard of so many women who tried to run a business after their husbands died. They always got into trouble. I wouldn't like to think of your capital going down the drain along with hers. I could do with the money, God knows. But I don't think it's something to jump at. I mean; it needs careful thought."

Bridget gave her husband a look to which he was quite unaccustomed, a long look which he found disturbing. It contained criticism. This was not the Bridget he knew.

"I am very sorry for Mary," he added. "When did it happen?"

"The other day. Your meal is in the oven. If you are going out, see that the door is latched. It was open for anyone to walk in last night."

Guilt and another feeling which on analysis might have approximated to shame kept Mangan in the hall staring at the door through which his wife had gone out. She had not banged it. But it seemed to be vibrating since it had shut behind her. It vibrated with disapproval.

Mangan shrugged. It was natural that she should be upset at her brother-in-law's death. Would she, he wondered, think differently about his request for a hundred pounds now that she had this assurance of good-will and money in the family? On the whole, he thought not. The O'Connells, whose money was so offensively and obviously plentiful, seemed to stand out as the source from which the money should be obtained. Mrs. O'Connell was using the play as a means to further her social ambitions. She ought to be made to pay for it. For the moment, Mangan forgot the considerable expense to which the O'Connells had recently gone. He wouldn't mind tackling the man. There was something about the man he liked, philistine though he was. The woman was a bitch. Pretty tough under all the affectation. The girl must be a throwback. Nothing of the mother in her. The thought of Maeve and, in particular, a vision of her, leaning over to reach for a bag on a shelf behind his head, acted so strongly on Mangan's constitution that, for a moment, he forgot the subject that had given rise to his train of thought. It came back when he compared what he had accidently seen of Maeve's figure with his recent recollection of another, one to which he had no reason to apply imagination, except for the purpose of transfiguration. Had Molly a hundred pounds? If not, how much had she? Perhaps Mrs O'Connell would be able to put up the balance. There would be no reason to tell her that Molly had made a contribution.

When he rang up, Molly answered the telephone.

"How sweet of you to ring up," she said. "I waited in all morning hoping you would."

"May I come round?" he said.

"What do you think? I have a chicken here. I will put it in the oven. What do you say to that?"

"Don't go to any trouble for me. I don't want you to go to any trouble. I will be with you in half an hour."

"How did she find me out, Sean?"

"She won't tell me."

"Did you talk, Sean?"

"Never."

"I don't like it. I moved from Tone's place. But we had a watch on it. She came up the morning after I saw her. Who is this Sandys?"

"The actor. You know him well."

"I have no time for theatres."

"But everyone knows him, Tony. He is a big name. I don't like him much. Rather precious. Frightfully suave. Why do you ask?"

"Is he the one?"

"The one?"

"The secret service man? Did he tip her off?"

"Nonsense. You might as well say Richard Burton is an Ulster Special."

"He may be, for all I know. I have checked on this Merton Sandys. He was a British spy during the war."

"I thought he was in some office, some cultural affair."

"Ministry of Information. I got all the facts."

"But half the journalists in Britain were in that. This is the sort of thing that was said about Erskine Childers. It's terribly unfair. On that reasoning my father should be locked up on suspicion because of his I.R.A. record in 1922."

"Don't underrate the British, Sean. This man came to Ireland for no particular reason. Within less than a week your sister learns of my connection with the movement and my address. And, if that's not enough, goes across the Border and lunches with him at a party composed of every thug employed by the Stormont junta. I look up this man's record. I find he is a trained spy. And you say it's nonsense. I wonder if you are a safe man to have in an organisation like this?"

"I've risked my life three times. That is more than you have, Tony."

"You will be sorry for that."

"I didn't mean it. I only meant to say you have no right to question my loyalty."

Kelly leaned forward and patted the younger man's knee. It was from him—as John realised—a splendid gesture. He burned with pleasure at the magnanimity of his chief.

John had been extremely anxious to find out the source of Maeve's information. Maud's reference to Gerry O'Brien came back to his mind. So far as he knew, Gerry had no knowledge of the organisation or of John's part in it. He knew, as most of John's contemporaries did, that he was an I.R.A. sympathiser, an extremist. But the extent of his activities was a secret which John had never told a soul. He decided to interrogate Gerry. Regard for an old friendship made John hesitate to mention Gerry to Kelly, he would not, at least, until he had tried to find out the facts for himself.

"You had better knock off for a month, Sean. You look tired and if there is any unhealthy curiosity on your account it will be as well to let it die down. Don't try to get in touch with me. When we want you we will let you know."

"*Slán leat*," said Kelly on parting.

"*Slán leat*," said John.

* * *

By taking Mr Kelly's advice John pleased everybody. He pleased himself because he could now concentrate on Maud without qualms of conscience; he pleased Maeve who was deceived into thinking that her admonishment had been successful; he pleased his parents who had not seen him in high spirits for two years: the extent to which he pleased Maud it was part of his business to discover. She met him for tea in Dublin. They went for drives together. In Horse Show week Maud included him in a large party to a ball. He went feeling shy—they dined at Saggart first—but excited at the prospect. By what seemed an accident Maud went home with some of the Mountstephens' guests who were staying at Saggart for the week; John drove himself home in chagrin. Maud had been gay and elusive all the evening. It had not been at all as he had planned. And her request, in a confidential tone, that he 'should be kind to Amy Baggotrath for my sake', which had touched him, turned out to be almost whole-time employment. Maud took her duties as a hostess far too seriously. She danced with retired brigadiers and her father's friends without apparent distaste: nor did she show any anxiety to relieve John of his burden, a stout girl who swallowed her sentences and did not shave closely under her arms.

Maeve excused herself from Maud's parties. She had an examination in the School of Art, she said, and it required all her attention. Molly Pratt rang up Kate to tell her that the play was on its way. There had been some hitch about releasing copyright. But that had been got over.

* * *

"I suppose two bottles of whiskey will be enough."

Dan was laying out supplies for the play-reading committee. "Anyhow it will have to be. Because it's all I have got," he added.

Kate was settling chairs and counting on her fingers.

"Milton, Merton, Francis Xavier, Molly (of course), Maureen (I don't know what she knows about plays), Maud."

"And if Maud is here Sean will be here," said Dan. "I can't make out what a boy of his age wants with a woman of her age. And I think the less of her for encouraging him. There's no harm in it, I hope."

"Harm, dear? What harm?"

"You wouldn't know nowadays what a woman like that might be up to. Sean has his faults but I shouldn't like to think he had ceased to be clean-living. I declare to God, I'd give up entirely if my children ever failed me in that."

"That one is as cold as a cucumber. I think the grandeur of her has gone to both the children's heads. Though John would have my life if he heard me say it. I am much more worried about Maeve."

"And the Sandys man, is it?"

"One minute I thought she was sweet on him. But now she won't leave the house."

"Don't tell me she has any serious ideas about him. I like to see her getting round and meeting a few people. We are not able to provide young fellows for her."

"If you ask me, she is daft about him. I am afraid to say anything. She bites the nose off me if I say a word to her. But no matter what she is, she is only human. And human nature is human nature."

"What are you suggesting?"

"Nothing," she replied quickly, and changed the subject.

"John is certainly a new boy since he took up with Maud. I will give her credit for that."

"Sean is a good lad, but too intense. My father was the same. Always out for principle. He wouldn't go to Mass after what the priests did to Parnell. It nearly broke my mother's heart. But when the bishops came out against conscription in 1918, he became a daily communicant. And he died like a cardinal. Six priests helped at the Mass. I wish my mother had lived to see the day."

It was so much a habit of Dan's to refer his two elder children back to his parents and to overlook Kate's connection with their existence that she had ceased to notice it. As the two younger children looked exactly like herself and spent much of their time with their mother, there was a measure of equity in the arrangement.

"Don't jump down my neck, Dan, after what I am going to say: but would you give up calling the boy Sean. It looks funny in front of strangers, you calling him one thing and me calling him another."

"This is more of your grandeur, Kate. Sean is a good Irish name. Why be ashamed of it? Why call him by an English name? This is the shoneen mentality that made us slaves. I called the boy Sean before we knew 'the county', and Sean I will call him till the day I drop."

"But you christened him John."

"Because that was my father's name. But John in Irish is

Sean. And we happen to be Irish whether you like it or not."

"The boy is much more extreme than you are, but he calls himself John."

"That's to get at me. He says I belong to a generation of cods who have bamboozled the people. He said that to my face. He said it was typical to christen him in English and call him in Irish. But Sean has very little interest in the language. It's politics first, last, and all the time with him."

"I saw Maud giving a look, when you came out with one of your Seans the other day."

"She may go on looking. And if she says anything to me I will tell her that she has come to an age when she ought to be looking out for a husband and leaving decent boys alone whether they call themselves Sean, John or Jehosophat."

Through the window Kate saw Molly and Mangan debouching from a tiny car. Kate could never cure herself of the habit of looking out for approaching guests. When they caught her at it, she never knew whether to disappear as if seized by an apparition from behind or to wave playfully. At Molly she elected to wave. Molly engrossed with Mangan had not noticed, but he had, and it did nothing to cure his ill-humour.

As though to counteract her eagerness at their approach, Kate did not appear immediately in the drawing-room, but broke in, as it were, upon them, looking ill at ease on the hearth rug, dangling tumblers which Dan handed round while Molly talked and Mangan glared at the portraits.

"You must take the seat of honour," said Kate to the poet, leading him to an armchair at the side of the fireplace. "And is that the play? At last. I can hardly wait."

Maureen MacLaverty was the next to arrive. She kept well away from Mangan. Maeve and John who had been avoiding their mother in the anticipatory period, came down from their rooms. Dan noticed that Maeve did not go near Merton when he arrived with apologies from Milton. Rehearsal trouble with the convent play owing to local teddy boys having volunteered for the chorus. He would, however, read the play that very evening and was most anxious to hear how it went this afternoon. Now only Maud was absent from the inner circle invited to attend the first reading. "I thought it kinder not to bother Mary

Kilmacud. She is so enthusiastic, poor dear. She would have insisted on coming. And it is too much for her."

Everyone was eyeing the parcel in Mangan's hand, and, at last, Kate announced that they had waited long enough for Maud and must go on without her. She addressed herself to John whose mounting gloom was ill-concealed. He glared at his mother, so that she turned hastily to Mangan.

"Let's begin. Are you ready? This is wonderfully exciting."

Dan, feeling self-conscious, retired to a corner. The poet fumbled with his papers, fumbled with his spectacles, cleared his throat twice, and began.

"*The Lost Heritage*, a play in three acts and six scenes. Scene one is a mountain road in the neighbourhood of Cashel. It is night time. Carolan, a blind harper, walks slowly across the stage, feeling his way with a stick. He finds a stone in his path upon which he sits. Then he begins to play a lament. A soldier in the costume of an earlier period rises at the back of the stage, a strong light shines on him.

"*Soldier:* Play on. I like your song. It brings to mind things that
I had forgotten. Warriors dead.
Famine and rapine, pikemen plunged in gore,
A once proud people driven from their land,
To starve in Connacht or to pine in Gaul.
Carolan: Who art thou? I am blind.
Soldier: And deaf it seems as well."

A laugh from Dan who thought a joke was intended had an alarming effect on Mangan. He threw down the play and banged his way through the furniture out of the room. Molly pursued him into the hall where their voices could be heard, Molly pleading, Mangan expostulating. The deserted audience sat looking at their fingers while Dan protested his innocence to Kate.

"You are not in the Abbey now, Dan. Why must you always be looking for a laugh? Go and beg his pardon. I feel so ashamed."

Dan, looking sheepish, dragged himself across the room. His bass joined the other voices in the hall transforming a duet into a madrigal. By degrees Mangan's voice dropped out leaving Molly and Dan in soothing accompaniment. The poet was standing out against them it seemed. But at length he allowed himself to be persuaded. The trio returned: Mangan sulky; Molly tearful, Dan mildly triumphant.

Mangan kept them waiting while he made ready to begin again. Molly's efforts to help sort out the manuscript were brusquely declined. There was an edge of hostility in his voice when he began:

"*Soldier:* And deaf it seems as well. I am not Hugh. They buried Hugh in Spain.
Carolan: O'Donnell!
Soldier: Wait. And him they slew by poison.
Carolan: Hugh!
Soldier: Not Hugh, I said.
Carolan: Tyrone!
Soldier: You weary me with guessing. Play again.
Carolan: What air would please you?
Soldier: Any, so you play.

"Carolan plays a lament. When he has finished the stage is in darkness. The soldier has disappeared. That is a short scene. Scene two is the hall of a great mansion. The tables are laid for dinner. Servants carry dishes. A great fire roars in the hearth. Sir Jonah Barrington in hunting clothes comes on, talking loudly, chaffing his guests. They are all in high spirits after their day's sport."

"How many of them?" asked Merton quietly.

"About thirty to give the required effect. What is the significance of that question, may I ask?"

"I was thinking it will be expensive to stage the scene. But, I beg your pardon, please go on."

It was six o'clock by the time the reading was over. No one had spoken after Merton's early interruption; but as battle followed battle, and troops of all nations tramped across the stage, and Dublin eventually went up in flames, it was apparent to all that the production would be a major undertaking. Carolan appeared in every scene, but his efforts to speak were always interrupted, and it was clear that his part was one for a musician and not an actor. The soldier in scene one was Owen Roe O'Neill. No one realised this nor did he make any further appearance until the end. Indeed this fugitive quality marked all the characters. They appeared always as ghosts coming and going without reference to the play as a whole.

The last scene, Mangan explained, was the vital link connecting all that had gone before. The curtain went up on an empty stage on the far side of which a theatre curtain hung. It represented back-stage at the Abbey after a performance of a contemporary, commercial play. Carolan is discovered alone. He proceeds to play a lament. Then a man appears in modern evening dress over a saffron kilt. He orders Carolan off the stage, in Irish first, and then in English. Carolan calls on the ghost of Yeats to come to his assistance, but no help comes. The sound of money rattling in a tin answers him. One by one the ghosts of the dead who have appeared in each scene proceed slowly across the stage while the kilted figure points and the money-box rattles. Carolan breaks the strings of his harp and follows them. The kilted one then recites a lament in Irish. And the curtain falls.

Everyone waited for the other to speak. The reader sank back behind his manuscript. Dan, when he was quite certain, it was the end, rushed forward with a drink.

"You'll need it after that," he said.

"It is very interesting," said Merton slowly. "A challenge to the producer. I wish Milton had been here."

"I loved the bit about the Earl of Clare," said Maureen MacLaverty anxiously. But no one supported her. Molly pressed Mangan's hand. She wanted to give him a feeling of support.

"Carolan is *made* for Christopher Casson," said Kate.

"You said that before," said Maureen MacLaverty who was tired of being snubbed.

"Do you fancy any part in particular, Merton?" said Kate with a tired smile at Maureen.

"I might double Pitt and Parnell," he said. "Pitt has no lines and Parnell always repeats the same one so that it should be easy to avoid confusion between the characters."

"Not your usual type of things, Mr Sandys," said Mangan. "I warned you I was bringing the writer back to the theatre. The actor must serve the play and not the other way round."

"You have brought that lesson home," said Merton.

"I hope so."

Mangan rose from his chair, brushing aside Molly's restraining hand.

"I am going now," he said. "And I want to make one thing perfectly clear. For no consideration whatsoever will I alter one comma of that play. You put it on as it is written or you don't put it on at all. I have refused to pander to the Abbey, either to its directors, or its moronic audience; and I am not going to give way on what is to me a matter of sacred principle. I have stood out against you all too long to capitulate now. And if you put on my play and they don't like it, all I will say is : I am prepared to take the punishment the mob gave to Synge. But I warn you; I am made of tougher stuff than John M. You won't kill me."

He delivered this harangue from the middle of the room to Dan who looked more and more guilty as the charge lengthened. When it was over Mangan gave a curt nod to Molly and stalked out of the room. She, signalling with her hands and eyes, followed him. The dramatic effect of this exit was impaired by Mangan returning and saying in a querulous tone : "Who will be responsible for the manuscript?"

"Merton has to show it to Milton," said Kate.

"I don't want to accept any responsibility," said Merton. "I should much prefer to be given a copy."

"It's all right if you look after it," said Mangan in a less unfriendly tone.

"I may have to leave it with Milton. Will that be all right?"

"Yes. Yes."

Mangan nodded farewell in a rather sheepish manner and made a fresh departure.

"His bark is worse than his bite," said Kate.

"I have no experience of his bite," said Merton.

"I could have killed myself for laughing," said Dan. "But I had no idea what class of a play it was. He will never forgive me. I can see that. I thought he was going to fly at me there when he gave out about not changing the play for anyone and all that. Why did he think I would want him to change it?"

"He wasn't speaking only for your benefit, Dan. He was worked up, I suppose. Well, what do you think of the play, Merton?" Kate had the air of a chairman who has formed his opinion but will not influence the votes of others.

"As a play it is out of the question. Even T. S. Eliot could hardly have expected to get away with it. As to its literary merits, I don't profess to be capable of expressing a worthwhile opinion. The end is intended, I expect, as savage irony. On the stage it would be pure farce. In fact the only hope for the play would be to do it as burlesque. But I hardly think that would please Mr Mangan."

"Molly will be fearfully disappointed," said Maureen MacLaverty.

"I don't see why we should consider her. I can't make out her connection with the play," said Dan.

"She is coming back," said Kate, whose eye, as ever on the window, saw Molly running up the steps. She had put Mangan down at the bus and hurried back to defend his interests. She had no illusions about her friends and knew that they were panting for the London actress and her smart play.

She heard Merton saying: "As a spectacle it would cost a mint. Do it against a plain back-cloth and you have nothing so far as I can see but a harp solo. And a pretty dreary one at that. One lament after another."

"Well," said Molly.

"Come in, Moll," said Kate with an affectation of heartiness.

"Can I get you a drink?" said Dan.

"What do you think of it?" Molly said to Merton.

"I was just saying that I'm afraid it's not a practical proposition for the theatre. That is no reflection on the writing. A play is a thing on its own. One either has the knack or one hasn't. I don't think Mangan thinks in theatrical terms."

"But there are wonderful lines. The whole theme is so inspiring. We have been waiting for something like this to rally round. The Abbey has turned its face against the poet in the theatre. Even Yeats is hardly ever produced."

"There is no action, no characterisation, no continuity and no plot."

"If it's plot you want, why not do Agatha Christie?"

Merton refused to accept this challenge. There was an awkward pause in which he looked quite imperturbable.

"It's very good of Merton to offer to act for us," said Kate. "I think we must consider his point of view. I would feel very badly if we had invited Mr Mangan to write a play for us. But it was really your suggestion, dear. Couldn't you tell him that we must do something with a part in it for Merton? I mean, what will the audience think if we advertise a play with Merton Sandys in it, and all he says is 'Beat up the Bantry Band'? They will feel we have let them down."

"With all due respect to Mr Sandys," said Molly—perilously near to tears—"the play will be advertised as a verse play by Francis Xavier Mangan. That is what the audience will expect, and that is what they will get."

"Be sensible, dear. They won't like it. And they will much prefer something with more snap in it and a part for Merton. I don't in the least want to make little of your friend."

"I won't allow you to talk of Francis Xavier Mangan as if he were some nobody I was trying to push. You are all the same, all of you . . . You don't want poetry. I won't stay here and listen to a great man being patronised by people who are not fit to clean his shoes."

"Molly, dear . . ." Kate began. But it was no use.

"I am very sorry about this," said Kate to Merton when the front door banged behind Molly.

"What's wrong with the woman?" said Dan. "Is she a bit queer in the head? I must say, speaking as one who has no right to express an opinion, there were a few bits in that play I didn't like at all. They were blasphemous. That's what they were. And I don't care who hears me say it."

"I expect she will get over it," said Maureen MacLaverty.

"Perhaps I had better drop out," Merton suggested. "I feel that I have been the cause of all the trouble."

The chorus of protests that went up at this would have convinced a more diffident man.

The question remained: who was to break the news to Mangan? A suggestion that this should be the task of the absent Milton was left in the air. Meanwhile all agreed that Miss Twigg should be invited to come at once. Merton had already sounded her, and said she was only too pleased.

"She has a novel on the same theme which she hopes to publish," he explained. "She rather fell in love with the Caribbean."

"We need hardly ask who will take *that* part," said Kate, who had quite recovered from the embarrassment caused by her emotional friend.

It was now time to go. Merton looked round for Maeve; but she was nowhere to be seen. John, too, was missing.

"Can I drive you anywhere?" said Maureen MacLaverty.

Merton was obliged to accept this unwelcome lift. But Mrs MacLaverty's invitation to luncheons and dinners in the near future on dates to be selected by himself, he avoided with a technique acquired by long practice.

CHAPTER XVI

DURING THE READING of the play John, seated at the door, had chosen an opportunity to slip away and ring up Maud on the telephone. His only reason for staying in had been to meet her; and he felt she had let him down although they had not discussed the rehearsal. Whoever answered the telephone at Saggart said that Miss Mountstephen had gone to London and would be away for five days.

A desire to vent his disappointment on someone sent John in search of Gerry O'Brien, whom he now regarded as a traitor and informer.

There was no mystery about Gerry's life. He could be found playing tennis, or later with friends who were assembling a motor-car from a collection of spare parts. John went to the tennis club in time to catch Gerry changing in the dressing-room. A pang of misgiving tore the wholly innocent conscience of that youth when he saw the tortured face of his friend.

"Hi there, Sean," he said, attempting to set the tone.

"I want to have a word with you, Gerry. Are you free now?"

"I am going up to Hegarty's place, as a matter of fact. I promised I would be there at eight."

"I will drive you. I have the car here."

"Fine. I will be with you in a sec. Would you like a Club Orange or a Coca Cola? It's all I can offer you, I'm afraid."

"Neither, thank you, Gerry."

John stood biting his nails while Gerry (who moved slowly) finished dressing himself and packed his tennis bag. He saw an unpleasant prospect before him and it did not encourage him to hurry.

Hegarty lived in Rathfarnham. John drove in that direction. He said nothing at first, but, at a quiet spot on the Dodder road he pulled the car into the side of the road, and turned a baleful eye on his unhappy friend.

"Have you been to the National Gallery lately?"

"Me?"

"Yes, you."

"What do you mean?"

"What I say. Have you been to the National Gallery lately?"

"What are you trying to get at?"

"I am asking you a simple question."

"Here. Who do you think you are? A guard? I am not going to give you an account of my movements."

"You met Maeve in the gallery. You gave her information about a certain organisation. This is known. I'd advise you to be careful. I am a friend of yours. But there are others who are not who might take a different attitude. I want to know: first, what you told Maeve; second, where did you get your information?"

"Well, if you must know, Maeve asked me to meet her. She gave no reason. She asked me where she could find you. You had been missing. I told her to ask Tony Kelly. That is all. I did not want to tell her, but I did. She was pretty upset on your account."

"And how does Tony Kelly come into this?"

"Come off it. Why become so pompous all of a sudden? Everyone in college knows you are in the I.R.A. And everyone knows Tony Kelly is a big noise behind the college cell. If you think you can keep a secret like that it's time you grew up."

"Do the authorities know this?"

"Don't ask me. There are Kevin Barry parades. No one takes much trouble to hide their views. You are living in the past if you think you belong to a little secret society."

"I had better tell Tony Kelly this."

"For God's sake don't say I told you."

"No, Gerry. Now tell me, who else was in the gallery?"

"Some very haw-haw friend of Maeve's who talked a lot to me. I couldn't understand what she was saying half the time. And a man who looked like Merton Sandys."

"That's who it was."

"Go on!"

"I'm serious."

"Who was the dame? I suppose all these actor chaps travel with a girl friend."

"You mind what you're saying."

"Don't get so offended. I always thought..."

"Stop always thinking. You will think yourself into trouble one of these days."

"Put me down, Sean. I've had about enough of this. And if you don't mind, I'd prefer to walk. There's no living with you nowadays."

"I am sorry. Forget it."

Driving back to Dublin after having left Gerry with two friends in a garage, John reflected on the difference between his friend's innocent and apparently happy existence and his own storm-tossed life. But his I.R.A. activity gave this satisfaction at least, that he could translate into violent action his dreams and desires. The new excitement which Maud inspired seemed on the contrary to be fraught with possibilities of humiliating frustration. The danger in this case was to his pride. And he was as proud as Lucifer.

* * *

Mangan had not referred again to the news from America, nor had Bridget.

In the turmoil of the play reading and its rejection (communicated by telephone to Molly) he had no thought outside himself. But after a stormy night in which he made Molly suffer all his resentment, he felt a violent reaction, a sudden weariness with literature and literary ambition, a longing for a break from a commitment which, like a love affair that drags on after its justification has gone, dressed itself in faded splendour, tapped a spring that had gone dry, and exhausted by degrees the nostalgia upon which it attempted to live.

Bridget was surprised to find him up when she came in one evening from the office. As a rule he was either out or asleep. But tonight he was in the kitchen.

"I made some tea," he said. "Let me pour you out a cup."

She thanked him but said nothing, waiting for the explanation of this change in the habits of a lifetime.

Mangan told her about the play. He left out Molly's part in the transaction, giving rather the impression that the play had been bespoken by 'a social gang' who had thrown it up in order to placate some actor from the West End who had come over to avoid income tax liabilities in England. It would be unfair to Mangan to suggest he was lying consciously. He believed what he said was a summary of the facts. In conversation with literary cronies he would have told the same story, but heightened the lights at different parts of the picture.

"Where did you get the money from in the end," said Bridget but without much appearance of interest.

"I came to an arrangement about that. It was sheer blackmail."

"I am glad."

Molly had given sixty pounds and Kate (without telling Dan) had subscribed forty. At the time it had been represented to Kate as an advance to Mangan. She saw it as the lever by which she might hope to ease Mangan out. She was accustomed to spend far more than that on a dress. But, for Molly, it meant the end of a projected trip to France in the autumn.

"I think you were right, Bridget. This play was never really mine. It cost me this disappointment to find that out. I am going to wipe the slate clean now. And when I write again I shall listen to your advice. You have more in that head of yours than I used to give you credit for."

"Did you borrow the money from that Pratt woman?"

"Did I what?"

"You heard what I said."

"I am not in the habit of borrowing money from women."

"Did you borrow that hundred pounds from her?"

"I did not borrow a hundred pounds from anyone, I would have you know."

Bridget unlocked a drawer in the writing desk and counted out one hundred pounds in five pound notes on the table.

"Give it back. I am not going to have that woman paying for you too."

"Take your money. I don't want your dirty money."

In an excess of rage which was partly simulated, cover for the abject figure he was cutting before his wife, Mangan threw the money down on the dresser.

"You don't. But she does. You are right, she can't afford it.

And if she hopes to keep you by giving you money she hasn't got, I wish her joy."

"I won't stand here listening to you, you . . ."

"Be careful, Frank. I want you to have that money. God knows I only pity that poor woman. I am going to my sister next month. I got a chance to take a cancelled reservation today. I am leaving you this place and all that is in it and I will send you four pounds a week from America. But life is short, and I am wearing mine away foolishly here. Good-night."

An overwhelming sense of grievance froze Mangan into silence. Humiliation, anger—both gave way to an all-consuming self-pity. He sat at the kitchen table, his face buried in his hands until two o'clock. Then he got up and looked for a half-empty bottle of whiskey which was kept for emergencies. He drank this neat over the next half-hour. Then in a sudden access of fresh resolution, he put on his shoes and started out on foot for Molesworth Street. An angry head came out of a window. He was pressing the wrong bell. He lit a match to make sure what he was doing. There was *Mrs P. Pratt* quite plain. He pushed the bell beside the label. Again and again he pressed it. Then he kept his finger on it for five minutes without releasing the pressure once. A guard who had been watching him for some time came over and asked him what he was doing.

"I am looking for a friend of mine," he said.

The guard caught the smell of whiskey that hung on the air.

"You had better go along home," he said.

Mangan drew himself up, on fire to maintain his dignity.

"Or I will take you in," added the guard. "Here, I will get a taxi. Have you the fare?"

Mangan rattled money in his pocket.

"Wait there," said the guard.

He came back in a few minutes riding on the steps of a taxi.

"Where do you live?"

Mangan gave his address, and the guard repeated it to the taxi-driver.

"You should be ashamed of yourself at your age," said the guard as he helped Mangan into the taxi.

His remark was a reflection on Mrs Pratt rather than the

distinguished poet to whom it was addressed. But policemen take an unromantic view of life.

* * *

"Who is that divine young man? He is scowling at you in the most marvellously sadistic way. No wonder you like living in Dublin."

Hazel Twigg, lying back in Maud's car, was enjoying her first glimpse of Ireland. She had arrived by plane that afternoon and Maud had met her. They were on their way to Saggart and had stopped at a garage to put in petrol.

John O'Connell, at the next pump, was having his own new car filled up.

"John! Hello! Come and talk to us."

But John ignored the call. He had opted for gloom. More desperately in love with Maud than ever, he felt completely at sea with her. Her changes of mood, her grand airs, and then that word which no girl he thought anything of would use. The English were decadent, on the down. It was plain to see. But she fascinated him, elusive and teasing, she challenged his manhood.

He drove away without looking at the girls.

"Are you sure you do know him?" Hazel said.

"I thought I did."

Maud was piqued. She had been away in London, and she heard that a Mr O'Connell had been ringing her up. Having decided to have nothing more to do with him, she rang John up after dinner and sounded coy. Why had he cut her? Hazel Twigg was longing to meet him. Yes, she had been away. Hadn't she told him? The trouble was he didn't listen. He was brooding over Ireland's wrongs so much.

"I am longing to see you. What are you doing now?"

"Nothing."

"Why not come out here? Everyone is away. Father found a cheap hotel in some broken-down spa in France and he has lugged Mother off there. He is recommending the waters to everyone on the strength of the cheap hotel. It's all such nonsense really because he suffers from high blood pressure; but his father used to take the waters and go to church, so father does the same although he doesn't believe very much in either. It will be an opportunity to see Peter. He can come up from the Riviera and quarrel with father for a week. He does it once a year. Very filial of him really. And he hates hotels and spas almost as much as he dislikes father."

"Do you mean it? Do you really want me?" John was in no mood for persiflage.

"But of course. You must explain the history of Ireland to me all over again. I find it absolutely fascinating. And I bought you a present in London. Don't get too excited. Not an expensive present. I have too much of my father in me for that. But still, I hope you will like it."

Maud was in her sitting-room in the tower when John arrived. She turned her cheek towards him to be kissed. It was a gesture unknown to him and, for that reason, fascinating. The girls he knew did not invite kisses, and expected on the mouth if kissed at all.

"I thought we might picnic up here off a tray," she said. "The dining-room is so gloomy, and there is practically nothing to eat."

But the tray, when it arrived, was laid with smoked salmon, chicken, salad, and a bottle stolen from the cellar, bought without the grocer's complicity, in a good year.

John was morose. Maud, appearing not to notice, rattled on about London, Hazel Twigg, the new play—nothing in her manner suggested there was any breach to heal. John found himself with a grievance and nowhere to put it. He must either forget about it, or manufacture an opening to admit it.

"I did not know what had happened. I rang you up. They told me you had gone away. I thought you must have been angry with me, that I had annoyed you in some way."

"How could you think any such thing? We had such an amusing evening and you interested me so much about everything. I have tried to remember it all, but I keep on getting mixed up. Who did what to whom in 1916? And why did they have to do it all over again a few years later? And who shot who? You must be patient and explain. I was trying to make it all clear to an English friend who knew ever so much more than I did, and whenever I trotted out the name of someone the English had shot, he said: 'But they shot him themselves.' I felt frightfully stupid."

"I didn't know I spent all the time talking politics."

"Not all, darling. Not quite all. But we did have quite a talk about it all the same. But I loved it. Why do you look so worried? I did love it. Come and sit here beside me. Don't sit like that on that hard chair. You look like a person paying a duty call. There. That's better."

She was a little girl playing with a young wolfhound, an incongruous and possibly dangerous pet.

She was smiling and he was tame, if awkward. He allowed her to lead him to the sofa, to fuss about him. She was laughing and talking very happily, touching him with her small, lively hands to stress a point, leading him, it could be said, on.

"Father locks up the cellar when he goes away," she explained. "I pinched that bottle of claret. But it's all I've got. If I had thought of it I'd have tried to get something on the way down. I know where there's brandy if you'd fancy that."

John did not drink as a rule; but he wanted this evening to borrow Maud's nonchalance, to be as different as possible from the accustomed world. He found the brandy quite hard to drink at first, but by degrees became accustomed to it. Maud, he noticed, seemed to have a practised hand.

As the evening went on, the room, lit only by the fire in the grate, became shrouded in a gentle mist through which he saw Maud's eyes, glowing now like lamps. Her voice, normally hard and high, grew gentler as it seemed to come from an ever increasing distance.

He found himself talking with an eloquence that he had never shown before. Maud's eyes seemed to extract a full confession of all the conflicts that pulled him this way and that, bewildering him, angering him, leaving him in a state of permanent frustration.

"Does it relieve the tension to shoot at policemen, you funny boy," she said.

But he didn't want to shoot anybody. He wanted . . . What did he want? It wasn't easy to say. Life was such a disappointment. You read about the glories of the past, but when you grew up you were told there was nothing for you but a safe job during the week and Mass on Sundays. Getting money, that was all. All the glory belonged to the past. Even one's father had had his, before he threw in his hands to pursue Mammon.

"Oh, do go on. I love it," she said when he asked her if he was boring her.

Then she asked him more of her funny questions. Had he ever been in love? Had he ever been to bed with a girl? Did he have to tell the priest about it? What was it like to have to share one's sins with a priest? Was it exciting to go to confession with a really juicy sin?

She asked these questions, but he didn't give her answers. It was her way of talking, he assumed. A sort of thinking aloud. But it made her closer. He had never expected such a proud-looking girl, brought up in a castle, to have a mind that ran so much on the things that even his friends got embarrassed when they talked about them.

Then she asked him to come over and kneel beside her in the firelight. She wanted to trace resemblances, she said. His face was not at all like Maeve's so far as she could see. Except for the high cheek-bones. And they both had lovely teeth. She asked to see his hands and took his great paw in her little one while she examined his life line and his heart line. This was an old game. Girls at rugger dances were always doing it. A chance to hold hands without letting on what one was up to.

"You will live to be old and you are going to have a very passionate affair, but not until you are middle-aged. It's something to look forward to. Now let me see the other one."

But John could stand it no more. He took her hand instead; and then, before he knew or had thought to do anything, he was rolling on the hearthrug, his arms around her, kissing her eyes, her ears, her hair.

It was only for a moment. Had she died then and there, the effect could not have been different. She had become so rigid, so cold.

"You jump to conclusions," she said. She was standing up then, settling her skirt which had got rumpled, and patting her hair into place.

"I'm sorry. I thought..."

He felt desolate, ill-used. It was as if he had been made the victim of a practical joke.

"You know I love you," he said.

But it seemed somehow empty as he said it.

"I don't like being mauled," she said.

She stood there full of cold hostility. He could say nothing while his mind made an exact inventory of every object in the room, each breathing its separate and distinct rejection.

He never remembered how he got away from that house. Afterwards he could only recall the various articles of unfriendly furniture and Maud, an angry stranger, at the fireside, settling her hair. Whenever he thought of her he saw that picture; that, and the moon's cold face when he came out from the cold within.

CHAPTER XVII

FATHER TOM SAID "Be careful, children" to a group of urchins swinging on a lamp post.

In deference to him they stopped swinging until he was out of sight.

He walked through the narrow street of Donnybrook, glancing at the shop windows and the newspaper placards and the motor-cars coming in to the city in a steady stream from Bray.

The Bective Rangers rugby ground where he had seen many a stirring match brought home the unwelcome purpose of his walk. He was on his way to see Mrs Kate O'Connell, whose patronage he found irksome. Rich and strenuously devout, she had laid Father Tom under a heavy tribute of obligation ever since they had struck up a holiday friendship in Parknasilla. To all the O'Connell family celebrations since that encounter, Father Tom had been bidden. In sickness he received presents of brandy and peaches. In health he was invited to dinner and consulted on a wide range of topics. Father Tom was a simple and modest man. While he approved of Mrs O'Connell's zeal he could have dispensed with her attentions.

It was out of keeping with his idea of the Church that an individual should claim so much personal attention. Kate, with her rise in society, had to have a chaplain as well as a Jack Yeats painting, a mink coat, and a house in Shrewsbury Road. Nor, compared with many who sought his advice, did Kate seem to have any problems which could not be coped with adequately in a confession box on any Saturday evening.

While he could not find fault with her for being so attentive (flowers out of season for the altar and all), he never felt comfortable when she consulted him. She gave him the impression that she counted on his having some back-stairs influence with God.

On the way home he intended to call on Mrs Mangan. This he had no appetite for at all. He liked and respected the little he knew of Mrs Mangan, and it went sorely against the grain to have to bother her about a matter in which he was sure she had excellent reasons to explain her conduct. But he had promised her husband, whom he disliked, that he would talk to her. Mangan had called late the previous evening and insisted on an interview. He was a little the worse for drink. This did nothing to mellow him but greatly increased his fluency. Father Tom had listened with great suspicion to Mangan's story.

"What makes you come to me? I thought you had no use for priests," he said when Mangan complained that his wife was about to desert him.

"I thought it was part of your duty to prevent this kind of thing—a woman walking out and breaking up a home."

"If I am asked to help I must do what I can, but I seem to remember you denouncing priests for interfering too much in people's lives. I thought you had no use for us at all."

"If you are not going to do anything, say so. I thought this was the sort of work you did. Otherwise I might as well have gone to a parson."

"You remind me of our landlord when I was a child in Westmeath. He hadn't a good word for the clergy and denounced Catholics as priest-ridden rebels. But whenever there was trouble with his tenants he used to come storming to the parish priest and ask him what he meant by not ordering the people to pay their rents."

"My wife is a great one for early Mass and the sacraments regularly and all the rest. But it doesn't prevent her, it seems, from leaving her husband. I hate hypocrisy."

Mangan spoke in the tone of one who will not be diverted from his theme.

"Why do you come to me in your predicament? How do you expect me to solve that for you if you don't accept my solution to the much greater predicament we are all involved in? And I am not your parish priest."

"Quibble. I might have expected it. Here, let me go. It is always the same story. I will call on the parish priest and see what he has to say. I thought it might be easier to talk to you. Your lectures on Catholic art and all the rest of it gave me the impression that you were more likely to understand. But I see I made a mistake. I don't even know the name of our parish priest."

"I will go and see your wife and listen to what she has to say and advise her. I would not like to think you called on me and I refused you."

"I am glad of that," said Mangan. "I don't know where to turn or what this country is coming to. There is no hope for the artist. Everyone's hand is against him. As for the Government—it starves the National Library and the National Gallery and the National Museum; it robs the money collected for the hospitals in the Sweep; it lavishes money on making the children illiterate in two languages; it lets writers and artists emigrate or starve and it keeps up an army—bi-lingual, by your leave—which could not hold out for five minutes in a modern war. It censors . . ."

"I will call on Mrs Mangan sometime tomorrow," said Father Tom, rising as he spoke.

Mangan was really addressing an unseen audience. He lumbered off down the street talking to himself when Father Tom showed him the door.

It was a glorious day with a blue-grey sky which suggests fine weather in Ireland, where a full blue sky in the morning must be counted with a whore's oath among the more fragile promises. Father Tom had to turn down an invitation to play a round of golf at Portmarnock in order to make these tiresome visits and it galled him to think of it. Perhaps, if he could get away, he might get in a quick nine at Milltown before tea.

Kate rushed out to greet him in the hall. Fulsome as ever, she was today plainly in a state of distress and excitement. But still she restrained her impatience to begin until she had done Father Tom all the honour to which he was entitled.

"Will you sit there, Father? Is the sun too much for you? Would you like the curtain drawn? Is that cushion in your way? Don't let the dog bother you. (Let me give you a more comfortable chair.) What will you have now? An egg-flip? Or just a cup of tea? You would prefer a cup of tea. Very well. I will ring for the girl." (After a discreet knock at the door and the appearance of a maid.) "Tea and some of the fruit-cake for Father Tom. And you can put a cup on the tray for me." (After the maid withdrew.) "I can't get her out of that habit of knocking."

Father Tom, allowed at last to settle down in peace, failed to catch the significance of this remark. He saw no objection to knocking on doors. Nor, to be candid, had Kate, until Maeve had suggested the practice be confined to bedroom doors.

Banalities were exchanged until the tea came and the maid went. And there was a further delay while Kate enquired about the manner in which Father Tom best liked his tea, poured it out, and waited to find out her success in satisfying his requirements. Then she pulled her chair in closer to him.

"I don't know how to begin, Father. I want you to talk to Maeve. Something has got into her."

"Maeve is a sensible girl. I am sure it's some misunderstanding."

"I wish it were. She flounced out of the house this morning after breakfast, after having as good as told her daddy and myself that it was her own business whether she married a Protestant, and a divorced one at that. I could hardly believe my ears. You should have seen Dan. Maeve is the apple of his eye. I thought he would have a stroke. And that is not all. John has been acting very curiously lately, staying away and keeping odd hours. He, if you please, started to go out with a Protestant, too —and she old enough to be his mother. I must say it sweetened his temper for a bit and kept him more at home. But he got into a terrible way, whatever happened between them. And to make a long story short, we haven't seen him since yesterday."

"And how did they come to meet Protestants? You always kept such a nice home for them here. I know of no children who had more done for them by their parents. And I must say I always felt they appreciated it. You have fine children, Mrs O'Connell. I am sure this is not as serious as it sounds. But I don't like the sound of it. Please God, and God is good, they will come out of it without harm. You will have to pray. And Dan must talk to the boy. A father must assert his authority. It's not the function of a priest to take the father's place."

"John has not got the respect for his daddy he ought to have. He's a strange boy. Three years ago, he got that religious he had us up every morning for seven o'clock Mass, and he insisted on the family rosary even when Dan used to come in late from

ridge at the golf club. He started to give out to Maeve for
oing to dances. That passed. Next thing he was at his father
or being rich when the country was poor, and kept calling him
capitalist to his face until his father reminded him of the
ourth commandment by clouting him with a tennis racquet.
Iow, if you please, it's politics. I'm afraid he is in with an
xtremist crowd in college. He doesn't talk much, but when he
loes he gives out to his daddy for forsaking the ideals of Pearse.
'oor Dan who did enough for his country in his time."

"And did he meet this Protestant in political circles?"

"Oh no. She is a friend of Maeve's. They met at a riding
esson at Dudgeon's. She's Lord Saggart's daughter. Maeve was
one on her. But lately there has been a cooling off. And now
ohn is gone on her."

"It's a phase. I wouldn't mind it. A woman in that class is
ardly likely to be seriously interested in a young fellow like
ohn who is no more than a student. Unless, of course, she is a
lighty one. Some of these society women nowadays can be very
orrupt. I think John would be well advised to keep with girls
f his own age and his own religion."

"We have to find him, Father. Then, perhaps, you would talk
o him. But Maeve is our real problem. She met this actor,
Merton Sandys, at Saggart Castle. I never thought a man like
hat would take much notice of a youngster like Maeve. But it
eems they have been carrying on under my nose and I never
noticed it. It was from something I heard outside that I learned
hey have been keeping company for weeks. So I mentioned it at
reakfast this morning, very quietly. Dan was reading the paper
at the time. She went as red as a beetroot, nearly knocked over
the table, told me she was old enough to decide about her own
ife, and charged out of the room."

There was nothing for Father Tom to say. He was in perfect
agreement with Kate, but he stressed his faith in the children,
their up-bringing, and their inherited virtues. He promised to
be ready for further consultation, refused whiskey, brandy and
sherry as each in turn was offered, and set out on his next
mission.

Bridget Mangan was less demonstrative than Kate. She smiled
when she gathered from his embarrassed overture that he had
been enlisted by Francis Xavier.

"I support my husband. I will continue to support him from America. He can get suitable work there. I shall never refuse him if he offers to share my house. But I must go. It's my last chance."

She said nothing else, and even the confession that she supported Frances Xavier cost her an effort. But if he was going to stoop to what he must have known was a sort of spiritual blackmail, she felt entitled to expose him to that extent at least.

Father Tom gave her his blessing, looked at his watch, and made for home. By missing luncheon and driving very fast in his car he was on the first tee at Portmarnock by one-thirty. He gave thanks to God. Milltown, an inland links, is stuffy on a day like this. Portmarnock, in the summer, only separated by sand dunes from the sea, is a golfer's paradise.

CHAPTER XVIII

THE THEATRE WAS full. For half an hour before the curtain went up no one could have doubted that such would be the case. The foyer was packed at quite an early hour with eager-faced chattering people peering from a vantage point on a step over the heads of the crowd to spy out less punctual friends or relations. The programme sellers were flustered trying to cope with the demands upon them. The cloakrooms were a rose bush of pink tickets. Boxes of chocolates were in request. There was a promise of much crunching and rustling.

To one familiar with the Irish, in particular the Dublin scene, the theatre as the audience leaped, scrambled or creaked to its feet for the National Anthem, presented an interesting subject for social commentary. The President sat in the State box with members of his family and his aide-de-camp. Ambassadors and Ministers accredited to Ireland did their duty in other boxes. In the front row of the dress circle, with their wives, Ministers for State sat with members of the Judiciary, an obstetrician, several tycoons and a few who were not immediately recognisable and were wrapped therefore in the greater distinction of mystery. From the stalls faces peered up at the boxes and the circle in interest, in envy, or in both. For it was an occasion to see and be seen. And there were many who felt hard thoughts because their menfolk had exercised economy or waited too long to get seats in the best place.

The O'Connells had a box at the back of the circle, which put them out of sight of those seated in the stalls but enabled them to see the play full on, instead of obliquely, as was the case with the ceremonial boxes. Kate O'Connell sat in front of their box with Maud. They provided a striking contrast: the older woman, very handsome, brightly coloured, in full bloom; the younger, less colourful, slender, inviting a more careful scrutiny,

and creating a less obvious, but more subtle effect—a Ruben
beside a Watteau, and both good of their kind. Dan sat in th
corner of the box, almost out of sight. Maeve, at the back, coul
only be seen by the very enterprising.

In the centre of the dress circle, but not in the front row
Lady Kilmacud sat with a dark young man in a bad temper
She had taken two tickets early, and avoiding the easy cours
of inviting a woman friend, had made a few casts for a man. A
the third she caught a very young secretary in a Latin-America
delegation who had but lately come to Dublin and had no ide
who Lady Kilmacud was when the invitation in an almost illeg
ible hand arrived.

For Kate it was a moment of triumph. Her family troubles—
John was still away—were forgotten. And Maud's presence, i
it added to the mystery of his disappearance, was at least a
earnest that he was not with her.

Maud made no enquiry for John. And Kate did not feel suffi
ciently at ease with Maud to mention the subject nearest he
heart before it—and everything else—was forgotten in the glo
of achievement, which she experienced as the flower of Dubli
society rose to its feet to the halting melody of the nation'
hymn.

The play had all the marks of an actor's composition. Th
parts were distinctive, the lines were smart. It suggested brillianc
as the smell of cooking suggests a meal. If the result was not a
memorable as the effort implied, it was because there was, per
haps, too much contrivance; and if the author had been as con
scientious as she was adroit the result should have been heavil
mortgaged to a score of distinguished authors or their persona
representatives. As so often with derivative plays, the structur
owed much to the despised author of *Peter Pan*. It is always wis
to borrow from the neglected. The dialogue was often natura
and where it wore thin there was patching from America
material. The wit was full of echoes. There was one daring scene
"They might have left that out," said Dan afterwards.

Maeve, blind and deaf to the play, devoured Merton with he
eyes. Every gesture, every nuance was like a fresh declaratio
of love. She found herself wondering miserably how much h
meant to the others, who in the past had seen him with he
eyes. And in the light skill with which he carried off an eas

part, in his panache and his charm she saw a future crowded with women blotting out the memory of a girl who had refused him.

With the thought of having lost Merton, other fancies came to torture her. She had never, for instance, considered him in relation to Hazel Twigg, whom he had described as 'an old friend', nor had there been the least sign of mutual interest since the actress arrived other than arose from the production of the play; but, tonight, Maeve felt a pang of jealousy sharper than any she had remembered in her life. It was near the end of the act, Merton had made improper but, in the circumstances, not surprising proposals to Hazel who, in turn, had made a proposal to him—that he should share his illegal earnings in the arms racket with her in return for her favours and her silence. She was not a sentimental character and the going in the Caribbean was hard. In this scene Merton made a gesture, a touch on Hazel's shoulder, casual and innocuous—but which, as Maeve saw it, told her with that instinctive certainty which requires no corroboration when it comes, that they had once been lovers. And with that realisation she felt a sudden hatred of the actress, a searing envy of the pleasure she had had with him. Her jealous flash passed in a moment and Maeve was ashamed. "From now on," she thought, "I shall be jealous of every woman in the world. I shall grudge him to everyone. I am a bitch in the manger."

But how could she approach him? What was she to say? If she just wrote and said she loved him and asked him to forgive her. Would that do? Or would he think she was throwing herself at him? It didn't matter now. She had no pride left.

The curtain went down to tumultuous applause. Kate swelled with elation, and moved out of the box to join the audience in the lobbies with the majesty of a sailing ship putting out to sea. Success did not improve her. She was not one of those diffident people who need to be driven on by encouragement. This was apparent in her attitude to Maud with whom she hardly deigned to discuss the play as they rose from their seats. There was something overwhelming in the way she received Maud's quietly spoken satisfaction, as though it were a bouquet from a child at the opening of a bazaar.

There was an element of comedy in it all which Maud did

not miss. Outside a small circle, no one connected Kate with the play. In so far as she seemed to be taking pride in the evening it was attributed to the presence of Lord Saggart's daughter in her box. But Kate never realised this. Her lines of communication led only one way. She gave out but she did not take in. Even when a few of her old friends, refusing to be snubbed, hung around until Kate introduced them to Maud, the older woman failed to see the extent of her delusion. Dan, who was never his best on these occasions, kept mopping his brow and offering refreshment to anyone in his vicinity.

Maud had tried to sit with Maeve but had been forced to the front of the box, Maeve disappeared when the act was over. Maud wondered whether she had gone back-stage, and was surprised on returning to the box to find her there alone. There was no time to talk to her now, but Maud resisted the slight pressure put on her to take up her place beside Kate in front. Now Kate sat alone, a brilliant solitaire, set off by the three figures in silhouette behind her.

The theatre orchestra was discoursing Mendelssohn's *Spring Song* without much conviction. Then the lights went out and there came that eternally exciting moment when silence descends on decent people and the curtain becomes the cynosure of all eyes as it is about to rise.

At that moment a man rose to his feet in the front row of the upper circle. He was bespectacled and wore a blue suit. The woollen jersey underneath served the dual purpose of a waistcoat and a shirt. It must have been uncomfortable on a summer evening in a packed theatre. His hair, like everything about him, seemed to be in protest against regulation.

He began to speak in a quiet, toneless voice.

"We are here this evening," he said, "watching a company mostly composed of English actors against whom I have no complaint. But it is, I think, necessary that this audience, representing government and social influence, should know that an Irish play by an Irish writer had been thrown aside to enable the performance to take place. It would not matter if it were not symptomatic of the indifference of those who ought to know better to the struggle at present being waged for Irish freedom by the few who remained faithful to the ideals and the sacrifices of those who had won the measure of freedom which we now enjoy. Some of these, until lately, had been imprisoned without trial by a native Government. It was not surprising therefore to find members of that Government sitting without protest while a play by an alien on an alien theme was performed in a theatre of their capital city by a cast composed of aliens. I will not increase the shame of those who are acting with them by mentioning their names."

He concluded with a few words in Irish calling on God to bless all present. He sat down in a silence which almost sang with embarrassment.

The curtain started to rise in a shame-faced way, but came down again when, from the back of the stalls, a young man in a voice quivering with excitement, but resonant and determined, proposed a vote of thanks to the speaker.

"We have seen a display of gaudy vulgarity tonight which made me think I was back in a provincial city in the company of an English Viceroy with the lackeys who cringed before their English masters."

"John," cried Kate in a voice of horror which rang through the theatre.

But John was deaf to his mother's cry. Resentment filled his heart, all the spleen in his soul was being vented now, the frustration, the fanatical longings of a turbulent adolescence all giving tongue at last.

"Go down to him, Dan. Stop the boy, for God's sake. We will never live this down."

Kate was livid, frightening to look at in her disintegration. Dan, standing at the back of the box, underwent the sensation of one who has been ambushed. Maeve leaned back in a sort of trance. It only wanted this, something as horribly fantastic as this, to complete her nightmare.

Maud, had John not been involved, would have delighted in the incident. The first speaker had lived up to her highest expectations of the native talent for solemn buffoonery. But the recollection of her scene with John robbed her of the pleasure in his case. One should not really associate with such people. She felt a sudden revulsion against this violent boy, all muscle and hair, with his eyes like a mad dog's; and as for his mother—'that dreadful woman'—with her vulgar impertinence! How often, for Maeve's sake, had Maud restrained herself from exercising her undoubted gift for putting the presumptuous down when Kate had made one of her hackle-raising gambits. And Maeve, on whose account she had endured so much, was she any more than a pretty, silly girl who fell head over heels for the first man she met who groomed himself properly and talked like a civilised being? Was Maeve not merely a regrettable weakness? Was it not time that Maeve pulled herself together before she was involved in some further indignity?

She glanced back quickly and saw Maeve rigid in the corner.

"Darling, are you all right?" she whispered, frightened by the girl's pallor.

She put her arm round Maeve's shoulder and supported her while the debate continued in the theatre. The lights had been put up now.

Francis Xavier Mangan, from the floor of the house, was disclaiming any connection with the demonstration. But, once on his feet, he was unable to sit down without giving a brief discourse on the decline of the Irish theatre and his own unswerving fidelity to the great tradition of Yeats and Synge and Lady Gregory.

Fear, let it be said, held back the management from dealing with the interrupters. But here and there anxious figures could be seen begging the demonstrators to be silent. No one apparently was prepared to take a firm line because to do so might seem a hostile act to the men who had illegal possession of fire-arms and a pious belief in the right of private judgement as to the time and place to use them.

Kate caught Dan by the sleeve.

"You must do something, Dan."

She had shrunk back from the front of the box, ashamed to face the audience looking, she was sure, to see how they were taking it. That John was not known to more than half a dozen in the theatre did not, of course, occur to her. Kate's temperament was resilient; but it had never been tested like this; and she collapsed like a tyre. Make-up was running down her face in which the lines were now cut deep, as she implored her man to work a miracle.

A massive immobility was Dan's reaction to the situation. Kate's social progress might well have been likened to the task of Sisyphus eternally pushing a stone up a hill. Not that Dan rolled down. He was that little much too heavy for his wife. She could get him to the crest, but never quite to the top of the hill. But now his impassivity looked like strength, and she clung to him.

"He will ruin us all," she said tragically. He had no plan in his mind. John's outburst had left him numb. In the very back of his mind lurked a grievance against Kate. It was her inability to keep quiet, her craze for society and prominence that had led to all this. If she were only content to live quietly at home, the boy would not have lost his head. At first he thought Sean must be drunk. Then he experienced a curious sense of detachment. This was a stranger. Not a son of his. Dan's amnesia was, perhaps, a way of acquitting himself of responsibility. Where had the boy gone to? What would he do next? Dan stepped forward to take a look. His appearance was greeted with loud applause by an audience greedy for further sensations.

"Silence," shouted someone.

"Say something, Dan," Kate whispered.

He was mesmerised, but years of commercial entertainment and company meetings had set up mechanical reflexes. Speeches calculated to smoothe and say nothing had become a sort of second nature. And like a man in his sleep he heard, as though from a great distance, a voice asking the audience to forgive an interruption which he was convinced had no other object but to stimulate interest in the Irish theatre. At the same time we had a national reputation for good manners. It was in jeopardy unless we allowed the talented performers behind the curtain to carry on. He was sure everyone was very grateful to them for giving their distinguished services for nothing. As to the play mentioned by the last speaker, so far as he was concerned he hoped that the Abbey Theatre, whose reputation needed no eulogy from him, would present it in the near future. He was looking forward eagerly to the prospect. But in the meanwhile, had they all not better see the performance that was ready for them? He would like to thank them all for their esteemed patronage of a worthy charity. Then, in Irish, he wished the audience long life and death, when that was inevitable, in Ireland.

The audience cheered and clapped. John had been hustled out, and now everyone was ready for the play to go on. It didn't matter very much what it was like. Everyone had had full value for their money. A crinkling of paper as chocolate boxes went from hand to hand intimated that the moment had come to send up the curtain.

Kate grasped Dan's hand. She had never realised his worth so fully. She felt as if he had beaten her thoroughly, something he had never done—to, she almost suspected, their mutual loss. She wanted a *man* to curb her fiery spirit. After what she had endured in such a short space she was glad to lean against him and take his large soft hand in her fat damp one.

He sat quite still worrying about Sean. Neither noticed that Maeve had gone. Maud, who followed, missed her, and now sat in the corner of the box, watching her friends on the stage.

It had been understood that there would be supper at the Russell for the committee and the cast after the performance. Vague instructions had been given to the restaurant because no one was clear as to who was host. Hazel Twigg could hardly be expected to pay for her own triumph: and the same consideration applied to Merton. But the committee as a whole had been a somewhat diaphanous body; those most active on it, with the exception of the O'Connells, Maureen MacLaverty and Maud Mountstephen, were not in a position to pay for anything. Maud, by virtue of her age and sex, could not be expected to make a gesture of this kind alone; the MacLavertys had never acquired the habit of disinterested entertainment; and Dan was tired of paying for everybody. No one, therefore, wanted to make a gambit which might commit him to anything definite. It was the sort of situation which does not arise when there is a backer who budgets for entertainment. The role of backer had almost been assumed by Dan because of Kate's ambition, but he had been at pains to prevent that impression going abroad.

The play received a tumultuous welcome. Nothing about it deserved the applause, in which there was no doubt an element of encouragement and apology for the extraordinary interruption before the second act. There was relief as well that the play had been allowed to finish without any further demonstration in the audience; but more timid souls did not wait until the end for fear of trouble.

The applause revived the spirits of the actors, who had been greatly upset by the protest. In London they would have understood it to have its origin in a feud between warring sects of angry young men, backed by rival theatre critics. They would have been annoyed but not alarmed. The worst could always have been anticipated. But this was no prank of a literary clique—that the rejection of Mangan's play in favour of Hazel's should be interpreted as a strategic move in Commonwealth relations astounded them. Hazel expected to be shot by a sniper concealed in a box. Abraham Lincoln's bearded face haunted her. The relief when all went well was tremendous. It produced an almost hysterical reaction. Hazel threw herself into Merton's arms when the curtain fell for the last time and laughed and sobbed like a school-girl.

Everyone wanted to talk. Representatives of the Press, operated by remote control, moved in with that terrifying combination of incomprehension and persistence that marks their kind.

"Are you in favour of proportional representation, Miss Twigg?"

"What is your opinion of the Casement Diaries, Mr Merton?"

"Do you approve of gerrymandering in Belfast local elections, Miss Twigg?"

"Would you say Beckett is a greater writer than Shakespeare, Mr Merton?"

Maud came into Hazel's dressing-room expecting to find it crowded. But the heroine of the evening, having shaken off the Press, was alone.

Merton swung round in eager anticipation when he heard a knock on his dressing-room door.

"Come in, darling," he cried out in his clear tenor.

Giving her face a quick go-over with her powder-puff, Lady Kilmacud waddled into the room.

* * *

Maud had supper with the cast. No one else appeared. There was no message from the O'Connells; but as Maud entered the Russell, she saw Maeve, looking white and strained, in the lobby. She was obviously waiting for her.

"Where have you been, Maeve? We were all looking for you," said Maud when Maeve, like a ghost, came up to her.

"Is Merton coming?"

"Yes, as soon as he has changed."

"Please give him this. I can't wait. You will see he gets it?"

She handed Maud a letter.

A group of people came into the hotel at that moment. Maeve slipped past and was gone before Maud could answer.

Supper was not an unqualified success. Merton was upset by Maeve's absence. He kept leaving the table and returning after a few minutes, looking worried. Only Maud realised that he was probably trying to find Maeve by telephone. Maud had not delivered Maeve's letter. It lay in her bag. There was, she told herself, no reason to consider it important. Maeve had not said so.

Nobody would have suspected that she was even a friend of Maeve's from the tone in which she discussed her with Merton. He was obviously on edge about her. Silly man.

"There is an unaccountable streak of violence in the whole family," Maud said. "It suddenly breaks out. Exciting to live with, I suppose. But one might grow tired of it. I like calculated risks."

"Do you really think Maeve has a violent streak in her?"

"I imagine you'd know that better than me. I've never tried to *rouse* it," Maud said.

"I hate you," Merton said with a sudden conviction.

Maud had a way of putting people off. She discovered it in her school-days and decided that her perception became too much for her friends. It frightened them. She didn't really mind. Unless, of course, she happened to have a crush on them. Then she suffered agonies. She had had a quiet special feeling for Maeve. There was no point in denying it. But she had fought against it because it was all too clear that she was wasting her time. And she had begun to suspect that Maeve was fundamentally commonplace, a pram and sink girl. Irretrievable. She blamed herself not a little for throwing so ordinary a girl in the path of this family friend at a time when he was probably over-susceptible. And Maeve was not fit for a sophisticated *affaire*. There was a puritan strain somewhere in Lady Saggart's family. It came out at times in Maud.

But even Merton's distrait manner would not deprive the evening of excitement. Whatever fears the interrupters aroused they did the work of an advertising agent for Hazel. Telephones began to ring before curtain-fall. A Dublin management wanted to keep the show on for a further week. The Press hung round the restaurant door like poor children at Christmas time. At midnight a call from London for an option on the rights of the play as a musical.

So rapidly does news travel that when Maud left the hotel, Hazel, in a corner of the lounge, was discussing film rights with a plump man who obviously meant business.

He looked surprised when the bill for a supper he had not been invited to share was brought to him to sign. But when he looked at Hazel inquiringly, she only smiled and said, "The food here is awfully good." He thought, then, that the supper had better be included in his expense account.

CHAPTER XIX

"ARE YEZ READY?"

Tony Kelly in the corner rose as he spoke. He was older than his three companions, none of whom had been speaking, but their silence was enforced by circumstances, his was habitual.

"My watch is crazy. What time is it?"

John like the others was wearing British uniform. His was torn below the left shoulder and soaked in what might have been blood.

"Eleven."

The four men, walking gently, came downstairs and out into a yard across which they walked abreast. The gate was open but they did not pass through. Instead they stood with their backs to the road, against the wall, and waited. Five minutes passed. Kelly kept on looking at his watch. The other three did nothing to reveal their anxiety, but John noticed that the red-haired boy standing on the other side of him was breathing heavily. Six minutes passed. Then they heard the motor-car. A few seconds later its headlights were thrown on the road. Then it stopped. The lights were switched off. The driver came into the yard.

Kelly now stepped forward.

"Ready," said the one who had come in. Then he went the way the others had come whilst they, one by one, went out on the road and took their places in the car. John drove, Kelly sat beside him.

They drove for ten minutes very fast.

"Slow," said Kelly. Then, after they had driven a mile or less, "Right," he said.

As John came round the corner there was a sudden series of explosions. Without stopping the car he raised his right hand and fired a revolver shot in the air. His companions each did the same. Then he drove all out. The road met a main road which led, after a few hundred yards into a village. There were lights in a few houses. Outside the barracks John pulled up the car with a screech of brakes.

"Hello there," he shouted in what could have passed for an English accent.

The car was surrounded immediately by armed constabulary. A torch flashed.

"The bastards got me," said John.

"Where are they? Come in, Captain. Where were you coming from?"

John got out and his companions followed. He feigned great pain to allow him to speak between his teeth.

"At the corner outside the village. They had a mine laid. Can I get through to Enniskillen?"

"Ring Doctor McGauran, Sam. Can you walk, Captain? We are going after these fellows."

"The wires are cut," shouted a northern voice.

"The firing seemed to come from behind the wall," said John.

"Would one of your men come with us?" said an officer. "I have sent for the doctor. He will be here in a few minutes. We must get going. This gang won't wait. Give Captain—"

"Jones."

"Give Captain Jones some whiskey. Help him off with his coat. Are you ready, men?"

John looked at Kelly and tried to read the message in his eyes.

"Sergeant Kelly will go with you," he said.

There were ten constabulary in the barracks. One stayed back, one had gone for the doctor and might return. The remaining eight now went off.

John had been at some pains to prevent the removal of his coat while the whole garrison was there. But now he accepted help. The constable put down his gun and started to pull the coat gently. At the same moment he was seized from behind, gagged, bound, and pushed into a cellar.

The raiders made a quick inspection of the barracks. Then they ran back to the car and returned with some parcels.

An attaché case was put on a chair. A charge was laid against the main wall of the barracks. Ten minutes had passed. No one had come. John stood sentry. The next few minutes were the worst he had ever spent. There was no sign of Kelly. No one was abroad in the village. All lights had been put out when the shooting began. Suddenly a figure appeared at the top of the street, swaying on his short legs as he ran. John went back.

"Come on," he said. "Tony is here."

One of the raiders lit the fuse. Then all three ran for the car. Kelly met them at the gate. Puffing hard, he got in beside John.

"Christ!"

The self-starter spluttered and was still.

"The handle is in the back," said the red-headed man.

"Then get it, damn you."

Two turns were sufficient, but John, remembering the fuse, was sweating into his eyes.

"They are coming," said Kelly, looking down the street. The car shot forward. There was nothing for it now but to hope that it would get past the wall in time. As they came round the corner of the barracks, John saw a child in the glare of his headlights. She ran to escape the oncoming car. He pulled the wheel round with a jerk which threw the car into a sharp skid. They missed the child by inches. She was running towards the barracks.

"The child," shouted John.

"Drive on, Sean."

They were past the barracks now. John slowed up.

"The child—"

Kelly gripped his arm.

"We can't help it, Sean."

An explosion behind them rocked the car, throwing John against the wheel. For a moment he lost control and the car mounted the footpath. Kelly made a grab at the wheel.

Then John resumed control, and drove as fast as the narrow road and the darkness allowed. After a mile they left the main road and took several turnings, ending up in a lane leading into a farm. John drove the car into an open barn. His companions jumped out and with the aid of a man who had joined them without greetings, they proceeded to pile hay over the car. The barn was half-full and it was only necessary to throw hay down. In five minutes the car was completely hidden. Then John and his companions followed the man into the house. A woman stood at the kitchen range. She greeted the party with a nod.

"I have the kettle on for yez," she said.

They followed the newcomer into a back room and took off their uniforms. John had cut his arm with a razor blade for the sake of verisimilitude : it had bled all over his shirt. Their clothes were in a cupboard. The new member of the party took the uniforms and pushed them into a laundry basket which he then carried away.

When the raiders were dressed they went into the kitchen. The woman poured them out tea, and there was some bread and butter on a plate which some of them grabbed and pushed quickly into their mouths. John took neither tea nor bread and he refused the whiskey which the host now offered round from a full bottle. Only one of the raiders accepted this. He drank it from a small tumbler defiantly, because he was young and the only one to drink and because, even in the tenseness of the hour, Kelly's manner of refusal—so strong is habit—revealed the total abstainer.

John stood in the corner of the room. His fear had disappeared. The pressure on his heart had gone. He felt only an awful despondency. No one had spoken until now except for the few words with which the woman had accompanied her ministrations of bread and tea.

"That child," said John, going up to Kelly.

"I don't know. We can't help it, Sean."

The host was a small man in his late forties, but he had the appearance of great age which jockeys have, a face in which the sap had dried from exposure to sun and wind.

"We had better be going," he said.

Kelly took out his revolver and looked at it.

"Will I take them?" said the other.

Kelly seemed to consider. Then he put his revolver on the table. His companions did the same. The woman put the guns in her apron.

"You be getting along, Ernie," she said. "I'll look after them.

"God be with you," she said, and smiled at the men.

Unkempt and prematurely aged, like her husband, by hard toil, she had a beautiful face when she smiled. All that John remembered afterwards of that evening was a woman smiling and a child crossing a road.

Ernie led the way. He had a torch which he used sparsely. He knew every foot of the country. The men walked in single file except in the open fields when Ernie kept a few paces ahead and John behind the other three. Sometimes Kelly glanced back to see if John was there.

On high land they saw the lights of motor-cars on the roads. Some of these were their pursuers. Ernie was able to make detours and to keep them from the highway, but sometimes it was necessary to cross a road. They crouched behind the hedge before doing this, then crossed in single file. Once they moved in a body but, on the other side, they had to take their turn and it was obviously wiser to wait under cover. Once, as they waited, they heard a motor-car approaching. It pulled up almost beside their hedge. It was full of constabulary. One got out and walked straight across the road to the hedge behind which the men lay. It would have been possible to touch him with a walking stick.

"Hurry up, man," shouted one of his companions. "What do you want to hide under a hedge for?"

In less than a minute the car had driven away.

After this the raiders felt less afraid. Their enemy, they remembered, was also human.

It was a dark night without a moon, but dawn would soon break. Ernie hurried on. Sometimes they saw the flare of searchlights.

Light was coming in the sky and the third cock had crowed when Ernie led his party through a cornfield and up against a small white-washed house. He went to a window and tapped five times deliberately. Inside a light struck and, soon afterwards, a boy came out. He nodded at Ernie and again at his companions. Then he led the way across a paddock to a small barn. A ladder was leaning against the hay. Here Ernie shook hands with the four raiders.

"Good luck," he said.

Each answered him in his way except John who had nothing to say to anyone now.

"Ye had better go up," said the boy.

The four men then climbed up the ladder. The boy went away but came back with bottles of milk and sandwiches, thickly cut, of bacon and cold beef. Then he took away the ladder.

It was a long day of broiling sun. It beat down on the corrugated iron roof. The men took off their coats and used them as pillows. The red man slept. Sometimes he snored. Sometimes he turned violently or muttered in his sleep. The fourth raider, a plumber, in ordinary life, smoked incessantly. He read from a newspaper which he kept folded in his pocket. He read very slowly spelling out each word to himself.

Kelly read Tawney's *Rise of Capitalism* in a paper-back edition. John lay back and stared at the ceiling. He refused the food but took some milk when Kelly pleaded with him. No one spoke. But, sometimes, Kelly put down his book and looked at John lying a few feet away. Whenever there was a sound of traffic on the road the readers strained to listen. The red man slept throughout the day, waking now and then, to make some inarticulate remark, then dropping off again. His sleep was heavily in arrear.

When the noise of traffic died away, Kelly automatically looked at his watch. The day was eternal.

When the light went the boy came back with more milk and more bacon sandwiches. This time he came up the ladder.

"They searched Ernie's place," he said.

"Well?" said Kelly.

"They took him in."

"Have they come to you?"

"Not yet."

"When can we go?"

"There will be light until after ten."

"Have you a cigarette?"

The boy produced two from his pocket.

"Want a smoke, Ned?" he said to the redhead.

"Thanks."

"Sorry," he said to the plumber who nodded understandingly.

"Sean doesn't smoke," said Kelly.

The boy went away. He came back in half an hour with a packet of ten which he handed Kelly.

The plumber took two of them, putting one behind his ear, and lighting the other.

It became quite dark.

"What's up with him?" said Kelly glancing out from the hay.

"Will I take a look?" said the redhead later.

"I'll go," said Kelly.

At that they all crouched down. A motor-car had pulled up

on the road, they heard doors banging and loud, harsh voices.

The men, who had lain away from one another all day, now leaned against one another, looking into one another's faces while they listened. All save John, who had not moved all day.

Vague sounds came from the house (a hundred yards away). Then the voices sounded again.

"They are in the stables now," whispered Kelly.

There was silence then, harder on the nerves than the noise had been. Where were they? What were they doing now? After a time the voices sounded again. They had moved further away. There was once more the noise of car doors shutting. Then the engine roared and gradually faded away.

With one accord the men fell away from one another, as if the string that was binding them together had been cut. Some time after this a man came into the barn.

"Are yez there?" he whispered. "They're after taking Kevin."

"Coming," said Kelly.

He got up and slithered down the hay. Redhead and the plumber followed.

"Come on, Sean," said the latter to John, tapping his shoulder. John like a sleepwalker got up and slid down the hay after the others.

"They took Kevin for questioning. Ye will have to go along the road as far as Tim Farrell's place. Keep close to the hedge. It's the third gate on the right hand side after ye pass the grocer's shop. Mary has gone up on her bicycle to tell Tim to expect ye."

The old man was plainly too worried about his son greatly to care about the strangers. He seemed impatient and clicked his tongue between his teeth while the others got themselves ready for the march.

"Good luck to ye," he said at parting, and stood, for a moment, at his gate to see them on their way.

Tim's house had been raided twice that day; whether this made it a safe hiding-place was a speculation. He was obviously used to these situations, and when the raiders arrived led them to a room at the back of his house as an hotel keeper would show his guests their rooms. He was a small man in late middle-age. He coughed a great deal and spoke very little.

"There's a flat roof below and when you cross it you can jump down into the garden. I have a bit of a ladder there that would get you into the lane yonder. But I don't think they will come back tonight."

The house had not recovered from the two earlier raids. Some of the chairs lay where they had been overturned. The grandfather clock, which might have concealed a dwarf had one been in the party, stood with its entrails swinging and exposed.

Tim had the manner of one who expects life to be dank. His cough seemed to epitomise his philosophy: we are on the edge of the grave and soon we shall be in the grave. He would, one felt, be disappointed if there were no injustice in the world to come. He was prepared to cough through all eternity. He lived alone in almost empty rooms. The floors were covered with dark linoleum. An iron bed, a table with a jug and basin on it, and a chamber pot in the middle of the floor comprised the furniture of the room into which he brought the fugitives. Over the mantelpiece was an enormous engraving in a frame of bird's-eye maple. It represented a Victorian lady seated under a tree, looking down: a man with a hat in one hand and a letter as large as the hat held behind him in the other, approached on tip-toe. It was entitled SPRING: and a bird, there could be little doubt, had once perched on the frame.

Tim had contrived a false wall which shut off this sombre room when the door was shut. The back of the door was lined with asbestos. Tim took no chances. The guests were not encouraged to leave their room more than was absolutely necessary.

Police called twice. At their approach, Tim knocked three times on the asbestos door. When they left he knocked four times. He came in with food which never varied, water, shaving equipment and endless pots of tea. He also brought in a copy of the *Belfast Telegraph*.

Kelly, as of right, seized the paper. After a few minutes of expressionless, but concentrated perusal, he passed it to the plumber, who spelled out the words slowly to himself, then passed the paper to the redhead who looked at it eagerly, then scowled as when he drank the whiskey at Ernie's. He was less complacent than his older companions, more at odds with himself. He threw the paper to John as if asking him to share his displeasure. The headline ran:

TEN YEAR OLD CHILD BLOWN UP IN MIDNIGHT EXPLOSION

John did not read on to find out the success of the raid. The headline swam before his eyes. He started to twist the paper in his fingers as if it were a rope he was desperately unravelling.

"Here," remonstrated the redhead, who had not finished reading.

Kelly who had been watching John carefully since the raid came over to him.

"Pull yourself together, Sean. Do you hear me? Pull yourself together."

John turned away. He did not hate Kelly. He would not have hated him had he been able to isolate him from the confused welter of impressions which made his brain swim and his stomach sick. He wanted to escape; but he felt that he was in a tunnel which narrowed as it progressed and left no room for getting out at the end. And there was no way to go back.

CHAPTER XX

"WHO IS THAT?" Mangan as always sounded as if he suspected a booby-trap.

"It's me."

"Oh. I called on you last night, but you were out."

Molly caught the note of injury in his tone.

"I'd have stayed in if I thought you were coming. Can you come over now? I've had terrible news."

"I am trying to get some work done."

"Later on then. Any time. I must see you."

The urge in her voice stiffened his resistance. He held her responsible for the fiasco his play had been. It was her interference with his affairs that had led to the whole miserable business; and he had consulted the solicitor whom he had retained in connection with the manuscript lost by the publisher in London to see if an action lay against anyone. But he had been advised there was no redress. This added to his sense of injury. Bridget's decision to walk out on him had been the final blow. He had consulted the solicitor about this also, and again without satisfaction. In the last resort he had turned to Molly. And she chose that evening to gad abroad. Now she had some trouble of her own which she wanted to land on him. Well, he wasn't in the mood for that. Thank you very much. He had enough trouble of his own.

"I'm afraid I'm very busy at the moment. I wasted all last evening going over to your place and waiting about for you."

"It wasn't my fault. Why didn't you let me know?"

"I'm not blaming you."

"Would it be better if I dropped over to see you? I won't keep you very long. Are you alone?"

He didn't like the idea of Molly coming to the flat. He never liked her to take the initiative where he was concerned. It made him feel that she was trying to get a grip on him, invading the proud independence of his spirit.

In fact he had nothing to do; and going to Molly meant a free lunch. It would also give him a chance to smell out the ground. Now that Bridget was on the wing he would have to make plans for his future. But he wanted to tread cautiously. If his wife thought he was hanging up his hat in Molly's place she might cut off the promised allowance. Women could be very vindictive.

What made him reluctant to go to the fag of changing his shoes and spending fourpence on a bus (and fourpence back) was an intuition that Molly's trouble, whatever it was, might involve him unprofitably. "I'll come over," he said at last.

Molly, looking bedraggled, her eyes red from recent crying, let him in. For once she did not fuss over him, but let him take the most comfortable chair without any prompting from her. She sat herself down on one with a hard high back.

Mangan was certain now that whatever she had to say was not calculated to cheer him. He braced himself for yet another assault on his peace of mind.

"Don't glare at me like that," she said.

"I wasn't glaring at you."

"You don't know what you look like when you have that sulky expression on your face. God knows, I have done nothing to deserve it."

She was showing her age. Round the neck especially. And crying made her look plain as well as woebegone.

"What's the matter with you?" he said impatiently.

She was crying again. But she pulled herself together after a few seconds, blew her nose valiantly and then, quickly, broke the news.

"A letter from a hospital in Bradford. Phil is there. Diabetes. But he may live for years. And he is almost blind. I'll have to go. I can't leave him there although, God knows, I owe him nothing."

Every word stabbed Mangan to the soul. It was as if at a crucial moment in a battle and reserve troops went over to the enemy.

"God knows you owe that husband of yours nothing. Has he ever sent you a penny? I'm not going to let you throw your life away for the sake of that fellow. This man and wife business is all very well; but it's usually a one-way street. And he must take the consequences of walking out on you. He can't whistle you back."

"He hasn't. The letter was a formality from the hospital. It's something inside me. I can't explain. But I know I must go."

"And what about me? Are you turning your back on me? Is this my reward? Who talked of eternal love and all the rest of it? Love, indeed! It makes me laugh."

"You have Bridget. She looks after you. I took Phil for better or for worse. I won't leave him to die like a dog in a ditch."

Mangan gave a derisory laugh.

"That's good. That's good. If you want to know, Bridget is going to America. We were offered a home by her sister there. Her husband died and left a business. She wanted us to go out and help her run it. Bridget is going; but when it came to the point, I found I couldn't leave you. I came round last night to tell you. But you were out. It was like a slap in the face—ringing and no answer."

The note of injury had crept back into his voice.

Molly, looking hideously plain, he noticed, her nose all red, stared in front of her.

"It's too late," she wanted to say; but she said nothing because she could never keep up with Mangan in argument. She just sat there, looking straight ahead, letting the truth soak in to him by degrees. Her decision had been a hard one to make. All hope of continuing such little pleasure as she had would go with it. But she would tie up one loose thread in the untidy pattern of her life, and cut off another. The future would be hard but it would be clean and clear.

They sat in silence. But she had her decision made, she had only to wait. His mind shifted about, waiting for a move from her. When none came the situation became absurd. She had no room for pity because she had been remorseless with herself. And there was nothing else to appeal to.

"Well, I must be going."

He got up and went past her, meeting her eyes with what he hoped was a cold proud stare.

He caught a bus and got off in Donnybrook intending to buy a chop on Bridget's account with the butcher there.

Standing outside the shop, Father Tom was waiting for his

curate who was driving him out to Portmarnock for a quick eighteen holes. "This weather won't last, we must take full advantage of it," he had said after breakfast.

He was looking forward to the game; and the sudden apparition of the disgruntled poet sent a cloud across the sun of his good humour.

"I hope all your troubles are settled," he said benevolently enough. Mangan had greeted him with a short nod, indicating that he was in one of his anti-clerical phases.

"I'm leaving. Going to America. I can't stand it any longer over here. There's some respect for writing in New York, and they've been at me for years to go over. They don't want me here. And there's no one left, only political gangsters and craw-thumpers. That's our glorious Republic for you. I've had enough of it."

"I'm sure the wife is pleased," said Father Tom.

"She agrees with me," said Mangan in a tone of voice that warned the priest not to intrude in his domestic privacy.

At that moment a car drew up at the kerb. Father Tom, with a genial wave of the hand, jumped in.

"That's the persecuted clergy for you," Mangan said half aloud. He had not failed to notice a bag of golf clubs in the back of the car. But he had other things to think about. He had spoken to the priest on the spur of the moment. He was by no means certain how best to explain his sudden decision to his wife. She hadn't spoken to him since he refused to go to America; and he knew her too well to believe she would ask him to change his mind. She was very down to earth, her mother having come from Belfast; and she had plainly written him off. She might even refuse to advance him the money for the fare. Women were unpredictable; and although he had lived off them all his life, Mangan had acquired no respect for them in the process.

But he would have to do something. He was not getting any younger; and the business about the play had made it clear that the last drop had been wrung from the literary sponge. Perhaps, in America, he might get lecture tours. They were said to pay. The trouble was, he couldn't concentrate any more. He had got to the stage when he rummaged through drawers looking for old newspaper articles, hoping to sell them again. On consideration he decided Bridget wouldn't turn on him now if he said he was prepared to come; her religion, if it was nothing else, would make her take him along. And her pride would not suffer. She would be saved the explanations to that sister of hers she would have to give had she turned up without him. But when he thought of himself in a foreign land at the mercy of both these practical females, neither of them with any reverence for his genius, his spirits sagged. It would have been better with Molly, bore though she was.

The butcher was quite impudent about the chop and wanted cash. Mangan was in no mood to be downed by a tradesman. It gave him a chance to blow his top a little. He came away with a cutlet and a feeling that he had won one battle anyhow.

Bridget took the news coolly. She raised no objection to his coming but refused to treat his decision as a concession. "Suit yourself," she said.

There were practical difficulties however. A very short time to get a visa; and she hadn't enough to pay his fare. She would have to write to her sister and ask for an advance.

"Hold on for a minute. I might be able to raise it."

He had been carrying on a correspondence with Dan O'Connell on the subject of his abandoned play. In spite of his solicitor's assurance, he still considered that he was entitled to compensation for his disappointment.

He had not asked for this in so many words, and Dan had pretended not to take the point of the letters. As a result the correspondence had been protracted. Mangan came from Cork and O'Connell from Kerry; the inhabitants of neither region can be matched anywhere in the world for circumlocution and evasiveness. It was like a courtship in the feathered kingdom, an elaborate ritual which postponed and lent dignity to an inevitable conclusion.

It occurred to Mangan that O'Connell, to get rid of him, might be prepared to put up the fare. With his wide circle of influence he might also be able to help to cut through some of the red tape in the American consulate. He decided to call, but later, in the evening, when he was fortified by a few jars. Not now, in daylight, in cold blood.

CHAPTER XXI

"HARD AT IT, Saunders, I see. That's good. But you enjoy it. Be lost without it, I suppose. Don't let me interrupt you. I'm looking for something to read."

Lord Saggart raised so many points so rapidly that the librarian was at a disadvantage. His own mind worked slowly and methodically.

"I don't like to see a great library like this in a state of neglect. It's the finest left in private hands in this country. But no one has taken any trouble over it in the last hundred years."

"It's very good of you, my dear fellow. My father took no interest in it at all. But he liked to come in here to hide from his awful sisters. He forbade them to put a foot across the threshold. He always had a bottle of Scotch hidden behind that bust. I don't suppose you have taken the same precaution. I could do with a drink."

"I'm afraid I can't follow your father's good example. Whiskey was cheaper in his day."

Lord Saggart, sensing the awkward possibilities of a conversation that touched on prices, let the subject drop.

"Thousands of books, Saunders, thousands of books, and not one that anyone in his senses would want to read."

"The library contains every book of note published in the seventeenth century. I was looking today at Clarendon's *History of the Great Rebellion*. It's in wonderful condition."

"I shan't disturb it. But you don't mean to tell me, Saunders —honestly now—that if you had as much time on your hands as I have that you would want to read Clarendon or any other of the tomes you have there. Tell the truth, now."

"It all depends. One needs to relax at times. I read thrillers myself last thing before I go to bed."

"I'm delighted to hear it. Well, in my case, I want to read

for relaxation all the time. I've passed the age when I want to be educated."

"One gets out of the habit of serious reading. I've dropped the classics myself. I used to keep a volume in my pocket. Horace or Catullus chiefly. Somehow I don't seem to have the inclination nowadays."

"But this library work is play for you, I suppose. I'd rather dig potatoes myself."

"I have a sense of duty."

"Duty! My dear fellow, don't ever do anything as a duty. Duty is what other people want us to do. The dirty work they won't do themselves. I haven't done what you might call my duty for years."

"Your lordship is singularly privileged. My duty is towards books, not people. The books will be here when we are gone. I owe everything to books. Very little to people. But I haven't asked what I can do for you."

"That's a polite way of telling me to go to hell. I only dropped in casually, looking, as I say, for something to read; but I don't suppose you can help me. It wasn't like that in my grandfather's time. He had a library of pornography that realised thousands at Sotheby's when he died. My grandmother wanted to burn it, but her brother—a parson, too, I'd ask you to note—advised a sale She intended to use the proceeds to restore the abbey in the grounds here; but decided to install a bathroom and a w.c. instead. Cleanliness, she decided, was next to godliness. Besides there was plenty of change left; and the restoration would have cost a mint. I'm always at the Government to do it. But they have no regard for national monuments. What could you expect of them, fresh from the bogs."

"You have a first edition of *Tom Jones*. Have you ever read it?"

"That's rather highbrow smut. I tell you what I'll do. I'll take a peep into Maud's demesne. That daughter of mine reads the most hair-raising stuff. It is all put down to the account of modern developments in the novel. It's extraordinary what women will read nowadays. And I don't suppose she has ever had a man. It isn't healthy. That's my view. They are learning about life at the wrong end. But when I tried to exercise my parental authority, she bit my nose off. So now I do nothing, and just borrow the books. Sometimes they are too much even for me. I don' know what the world's coming to. Do you, Saunders? What d you make of it? You are a brainy fellow. You must have thought on the subject."

The librarian shifted uneasily in his chair, smiled wanly an then frowned at his boots.

"I don't think my reflections are of much value. I have ver little time for it. I . . ."

He glanced down desperately at the catalogue from which thi dirty-minded old miser was detaining him.

"I'm so behind in my work. I had hoped to get this don before Christmas. But now I shan't be able to."

"Take it easy, old man. All work and no play, you know, wa never good for either man or beast. Don't keep your nose in th books all the time. Make yourself at home here. They have television downstairs. That sinister Italian couple wouldn't stay they said, if I didn't get them one. I go down there very ofte and look in. They don't seem to mind. If there's any programm you fancy, I'm sure they will let you in to look at it."

Mr Saunders murmured thanks but showed no anxiety to ac on the kind suggestion. Lord Saggart raised himself from th Recamier sofa on which he was taking his ease. He gave a grea shake, as a dog does when it comes out of water, and then smiling slyly as his habit was, strode out of the room withou any signal of departure.

Maud had a tower in the castle to herself. Her father, wh seldom came in, looked around and sniffed. On the table la *The Nun of Monza.* His lordship took a quick glance throug the pages, looking more than ever like a hound on the scen He had an unerring instinct for smut; and some of these page looked highly seasoned. The idea in association with nuns wa pleasing, too. He was well satisfied. Perhaps Maud should b told to help Saunders. She would certainly enliven the collectio He went back to report his find to the librarian.

Did he hear Mr Saunders' little sigh when he put his big fac round the door? It was never easy to know what he paid hee to.

"What did I tell you? This looks rather spicy."

Mr Saunders looked politely at the volume.

"This is based on historical records," he said approvingly.

"I don't care about that so long as it has something I can get my teeth into. What's that?"

A letter had fallen out of the book.

Mr Saunders picked it up.

"It's addressed to Mr Merton Sandys," he said.

"Maud must have forgotten to post it. Sandys is the actor fellow who was staying here."

"I met Mr Sandys."

The librarian's tone was reproving. There was nothing he disliked more in Lord Saggart than the way in which he overlooked one if he didn't want anything.

"That's not Maud's writing. It's a woman's hand, though. Looks as if we've tumbled on to something, Saunders. Is Maud acting as a go-between?"

"I will post it when I'm in the village," Mr Saunders said. "But I see it isn't addressed. We can look it up in *Who's Who*."

"Just post it as it is. I'll bet you a fiver—no, not a fiver, sixpence. I bet you sixpence it will find him."

Mr Saunders looked troubled. It seemed wrong to him to put a letter to such hazard.

"And I wouldn't waste a stamp on it either. I've always been told it's the best way to insure delivery. The Post Office is so greedy for money it pursues the fellow at the other end so as to make sure it gets paid by somebody."

"But they are charged double."

"That actor fellow can well afford it. Let's hope it's worth it. A fan letter, I expect. But I can't see Maud writing fan letters. Bloody silly anyway when she knows the fellow."

"But you said it wasn't Miss Mountstephen's writing."

"Neither is it, by God! Well, then it would be mad to waste a stamp on it. I'll be off. I think I'm going to enjoy this book. Chap in it is going round the convent like a rooster. The climate has a lot to do with it."

A quarter of an hour later, Lord Saggart interrupted his reading to think of the letter addressed to 'Merton Sandys, Esq.' starting off on its unfranked journey round the earth. The idea tickled his labyrinthine sense of humour. He began to laugh; and as his fertile fancy conjured up one hazard after another ending with the actor's firm refusal to accept a letter upon which he had to pay, Lord Saggart's laughter grew even wilder and more free. It penetrated even the library door. Mr Saunders frowned. There was nobody whom he disliked so cordially as he did his lordship.

Methodically he got down *Who's Who* (last year's copy bought at a reduction).

"Merton Sandys," he read, "Actor, Born 26th February 1922. O.S. of Rev. Quintin Sandys, D.D., Bishop of Lahore."

There was no address given other than a bank.

Mr Saunders wrote that neatly on the envelope and then 'Please forward' on the top, right-hand corner. Then he took out his note case in which he kept a book of stamps, and with a resigned sigh, affixed one. The next collection was at four o'clock p.m. he noticed as he dropped the letter in the green pillar box at the corner.

CHAPTER XXII

"YOU'LL HAVE TO go without me," Kate said. "I can't leave the child in the condition he's in."

"We're ten minutes late as it is," Dan said.

"Ring up and say that one of the children is ill; and they'll have to excuse me."

"But they know Sean is twenty-one. Do you want to make a laughing stock of us?"

"You saw how he was yourself. He won't let me leave him. And he won't let me get the doctor. By the same token I think you might give Dr Burke a call some time and explain the situation. There might be some class of sleeping pill he'd recommend."

"I don't know what's got into the boy," Dan said. Then he added, "Would you ring up Mrs Brennan yourself and explain? I can be getting along. The Minister has been so civil lately, I don't want to spoil it all on account of Sean's carry-on."

Dan had a vague notion of the cause of his son's return in a broken-down condition after an unexplained absence. He had not been seen since the scene in the theatre; that had made plain enough the explanation of his erratic behaviour. He was in with the wrong lot.

Dan had promised his wife to call on the President of the college and have it out with him. He had heard from several sources that a Republican group was active among the students. How the President could help was by no means clear; but Kate was a great believer in communications at the highest level on all topics that concerned the family. It was important to emphasise the fact of one's importance and refuse to accept any run of the mill treatment.

But the scene in the theatre had had a quite unexpected effect. It had drawn attention to an aspect of Dan's career that was well-nigh forgotten. Nowadays people thought of him as a tycoon and forgot his revolutionary past. Not that there was much in it; a bomb thrown over a wall at a car that missed its mark. That was the only action in which he had been engaged. But it blooded him. And he had worn uniform in the Civil War. His close connection with Michael Collins was a legend, founded on a myth. On the only occasion they had met, Collins had told him to "get to Hell out of that". But there were no witnesses. And the leader was suffering under strain. Since Collins's death, his devotion to Dan was accepted as part of Ireland's history. It had made Dan in business.

A few days after the theatre scene, a third party had let Dan know that the Minister, Patrick Brennan, would like to attend the firm's annual dinner. This had made quite a stir and the Press was generous in its coverage. When Ministers went to dinners they used the occasion to foreshadow policy. At Dan's dinner the guests sat for an hour listening to the prospects of using horse manure in a national mushroom industry. Before he sat down the Minister eulogised Dan in a particularly striking manner, as one who had "answered Ireland's call in her darkest days", as a man "in whose heart the proudest traditions of the Gael had a special place", as one who if the tocsin were ever to sound again would "leap into the breach". He extolled Dan's "prudent and patriotic" career in industry and claimed that as a patron of the arts he was known "beyond the narrow confines of this ancient nation".

It was all very pleasant and surprising, particularly because through the years Dan had rather disliked Paddy Brennan and had no reason to believe the antipathy was not mutual. The Kerryman in him enquired what was behind it all; and when the Minister rang him up to say it was a long time since they had had a chat, and would he and his missus come round for a quiet bite with Maureen and himself, Dan knew that there was a purpose and it would be disclosed at the dinner. He hoped it would not be a request for funds for the party.

On the day of this meeting Sean turned up, giving no explanation of his absence, but clearly very much the worse for wear. He had clung to his mother and sobbed like a child. That was ten hours ago.

The idea had crossed Dan's mind to take Maeve to the dinner in her mother's place. He was inordinately proud of her and liked to show her off. But Maeve had not shown up since lunch time. She had been very quiet and mysterious lately in her manner.

Dan dated all his troubles back to the day Kate had involved the family in the anti-rheumatism campaign. That affliction seemed a mild one to have to bear in comparison with what he had put up with; huge expense, undesirable publicity and a total transformation of his daughter's character.

As he was opening the hall door he saw an envelope in the letterbox. He put it in his pocket not having time to read it then.

The Minister was all over him when he arrived. Kate's absence was obviously no matter for disappointment. Dan was treated like an old friend of the family; and if the hired waiter robbed the occasion of the domestic informality he had been promised, Mrs Brennan mixed him a bumper of Gaelic coffee with her own unaccustomed hands.

Then she retired and the Minister produced cigars. It was coming now, whatever it was. Dan fixed his eyes on his glass and gently twiddled the stem.

"Have you ever thought of yourself in the Park?" the Minister said.

"In the Park?"

Hardly able to take in the significance of the question, his heart beating with a wild surmise, Dan had played for time.

"Why not? Who is better entitled? You'll keep this under your hat of course. This is strictly off the record; but the fact is the Presidential election will be coming off fairly soon, and we must be prepared well in advance. Some of my colleagues have expressed the view that we ought to try and get an agreed candidate on the next occasion. It doesn't do anyone any good to have the Presidential election turned into a political dog-fight. The President is supposed to be above politics."

"But you don't have a dog's chance of being elected if you're not a politician."

"Right. But if we can approach the other side with someone they don't object to, who hasn't a party label and yet is eligible, it might be wise. For a change, I mean. And to be quite honest, I'm nervous about our chances next time with our own man. He might well be beaten."

Kate in one of her more euphoric moments had told Dan that he ought to consider an approach to one party or the other on this very question. But he lacked her drive; and he did not like asking for favours that might be refused. Kate was less sensitive on this score.

His vanity was flattered now. He felt quite heady. The very suggestion had somehow enlarged him. If in the abstract he felt unworthy of the honour, now that it was a possibility he grew in his own estimation. He seemed to be displacing more air. Even the fingers with which he continued to twist the glass took on a more significant look. Everything about him counted for more. And he thought of Kate. The trouble would be restraining her. She would burst out of the paddock, and no mistake, when she heard the news. There would be no holding her now.

"It would be a terrible wrench. I'm not fond of formalities, and my business has become my life. I've the children to think of. But if you think that I can serve the country well . . ."

"A devil a bit of harm it will do the business, Dan. But you had better keep this to yourself until I see the Cabinet again. If the other crowd get an inkling of what we are doing they'll forestall us with some tame cat of their own."

"Who is there?" said Dan, suddenly feeling a challenge.

"They'll dig up some old judge or some literary fellow. One of these writers might do wonders for the tourist trade."

"They are usually a bit tricky on the moral side."

"Age works wonders in that department."

"Are you sure I'm the right man?"

"You know me, Dan. I wouldn't waste time talking to you if I thought you weren't. But you must make up your mind quickly. We want to put this thing through before the end of the session."

Dan drove home in a haze. He would not be able to resist telling Kate. Perhaps the news might bring Sean to his senses. The boy had a heart in him, and he must be proud to think his father would be the first man in the land.

He wished his own mother were alive to see him now. When the car arrived at Tara, tears were in Dan's eyes. Thrusting his hand into the side pocket of his overcoat where he usually kept a handkerchief, he felt the stiff edge of the envelope he had picked up on his way out.

He took it up and glanced at it casually. It was in Maeve's

handwriting. He had not noticed it before. He opened it with a faint foreshadowing of bad tidings. Why would Maeve write to him?

Darling Dad,
I know it will hurt you. I'm sorry. I don't want to. I'm on my way to Spain to join Merton. We will get married when his divorce comes through. Don't try to stop me. I won't leave him. Tell Mummy. I'm sorry if I hurt you. I didn't want to.

Your sad and loving daughter
Maeve.

He read the letter over many times, as if he could read the message off the page. Then he crumpled it up into a ball in his broad palm. Then he pushed this back in his pocket and walked very slowly up the steps to his hall door. Someone was standing in the shadows.

"Mr O'Connell."

He didn't answer. He had lost his own identity.

"I'm sorry to come round so late, but I was told you were out at dinner. It's urgent, or I wouldn't disturb you now. I'm sure you want to get to bed."

Dan struggled to relate all this to the only topic in his mind. It was easier to open the hall door than to talk to this caller. By family custom the key was left in the lock when one was out and the other at home. He stepped in and his visitor followed him.

Now in the light of the hall Dan recognised the poet, Mangan. Everything clicked into place. The play, the actor, Maureen. This fellow had been wearing him out with insinuating blackmailing letters. Why had he come now?

Mangan looking up into his troubled eyes did not realise that the mind behind them was playing with the idea of picking him up and hurling him down the steps.

"Is that you, Dan?"

Kate's voice sounded from the stairs.

It saved Mangan's life. At the sound of his wife's voice another combination was substituted for that which logically ended in Mangan's execution.

Kate, Paddy Brennan, the Presidency.

And did that combination not begin with Mangan's play?

"He's gone to the guards," said Kate, ignoring Dan's companion. "He's given himself up. He pretended to be asleep; and I like a fool left him alone. The inspector rang up just now to tell me. He said you might want to get a solicitor. Sean wants to make a statement."

Her voice broke on this; and with the vehemence with which she did everything, she threw herself sobbing wildly on to Dan's chest.

He held her there, unheeding, as if she were a parcel he had been handed, while his mind tried to work out its course. He had drunk the best part of a bottle of liqueur whisky during the evening.

A son in prison, a daughter in the divorce court, a nice start for a Presidental candidate! But what did the Presidency matter? He had lost Maeve, his darling Maeve, his little girl, his most precious treasure. What the hell about the rest.

The mist began to recede. Action was called for. He would go back to see Brennan and tell him about Sean. There might be time to get him out of the mess. Brennan could do it.

"I'm very sorry for coming at such a time," said Mangan.

Dan surveyed him. The mist was receding fast. He was at his best his colleagues knew in an emergency.

"Come with me, Mangan," he said. "I am going to see the Minister."

"He won't want to see me," said the poet. He had realised from the time they entered the hall that Dan had been drinking.

"Oh yes he does. He wants to see you very badly. He wants you to stand for the Presidency. A literary man. That's what the country wants. The other crowd will dig one up if we don't."

Mangan followed him down the steps, and climbed into the car apprehensively. He was not quite sure that Dan was fit to drive. But he didn't really care very much. A strange excitement lifted him above practical considerations. For once, he did not question motives or suspect some design of low cunning. Dan had convinced him. It had been a remarkable half hour. The headlights of the car as it turned out on the road lit up the name in gold letters on the gate post. TARA.